HE'S APPARENTLY
A REALLY BIG DILL.

big

PICKLE

JJ KNIGHT

The *USA Today* bestselling author of

Single Dad on Top
The Accidental Harem
Uncaged Love
Fight for Her
Reckless Attraction

Want to make sure you don't miss a release?
Join JJ's email or text list.

Edition 1.1

Casey Shay Press
PO Box 160116
Austin, TX 78716
www.jjknight.com

Paperback ISBN: 9781938150906

1

JACE

It's pretty great when a new Pickle comes into the world.

Today my cousin Greta is giving birth.

Like, literally, right now.

She's walking the halls and refuses to lie in bed.

Her husband Jude is off talking to the doctor, hoping they can convince Greta to lie down and accept an epidural.

Her pain is great. She's already cussed out all the nurses.

But Greta hates needles. This is a fear we share.

Since I'm on her side, Greta asks me to walk the halls with her to escape the hostility. She stops every few minutes to let out a rather alarming groan.

I've texted both my brothers *and* my dad to walk with me because I have this terrible, awful feeling my cousin is going to squeeze out a kid on the linoleum floor.

And it'll be my fault.

They'll say since I hated needles and spouted off about how horrible they were when we were kids, that I'm the one who poisoned Greta on them.

And that's why she's currently walking the halls of Mercy Hospital, deep into labor pains, and refusing to even put in an IV.

It's on me.

Totally.

I'm the eldest of all the cousins. I'm the big Pickle.

I was a tyrant in our youth. I made everybody listen to me. Follow my lead. Do what I say.

Especially when needles were involved. I provided detailed descriptions of the pediatrician's office, so the cousins knew where to flee when the vaccine shot came out.

And here we are. Still on the run.

Greta's wheat-blond hair sticks to her forehead in sweaty clumps. She wears two blue hospital gowns, one open to the back and one to the front, to avoid having to worry about drafts.

I hold her arm as we walk along the hall, the occasional visitor looking at us with alarm as they pass.

"Maybe needles aren't that bad—" I venture.

She cuts me off. "Shut up, Jace. I'm trying to have a baby here."

"Wouldn't it be better in bed? With sheets? And a doctor?"

"Walking helps labor go faster."

"We've been walking half an hour—"

"Shut up, Jace!"

I shut up.

We make it a few more steps when suddenly, Greta's face goes red, she bends over, and squats smack in the middle of the hall.

The groan that comes out of her mouth would scare off a pride of mountain lions.

I look around frantically for a doctor, a nurse, a janitor. Anybody.

Why is nobody outside their rooms?

We're at least ten miles from the nursing station.

"You okay, Greta?"

She huffs in several big breaths. "I think he's coming!"

"What!"

She lets out another long screech and I do the only thing I can think of, harkening back to my football days.

I lunge to the floor between her legs and hold out my hands to make the catch.

My brother Max got a picture.

Of course he did.

While Greta holds baby Caden, who was born quite properly in her bed a solid hour after my baby dive, Max uploads the shot of me on the floor, my hands outstretched beneath the hem of my cousin's gown, to his Instagram.

I'm going to kill him.

But not in front of the baby.

He and my youngest brother Anthony snicker over it endlessly.

Bastards.

We're about to get in a shoving match like we're twelve instead of pushing thirty, when the great matriarch of the family, Grammy Alma comes in.

"Boys, behave," she orders.

We stand still like we always do.

"Let me see that child." Grammy moves to the bed, her orthopedic shoes squeaking on the floor. She's spry for eighty, and still runs the original deli of the Pickle clan, deep in the heart of Queens. My other cousin Sunny helps her.

Delis definitely run in the Pickle blood. My dad owns the massive Manhattan Pickle, which takes up an entire city block. As each of the three Pickle sons ventured off for college, he built a franchise for us in our chosen towns.

Anthony is the baby of the brothers. He's dressed casually in jeans and a T-shirt that reads "Another one bites the crust." He's twenty-six and runs the deli in Boulder, where he went to culinary school.

Max, our middle brother, is two years younger than me. He is undoubtedly the alpha. He's a workout junkie, and he's tricked-out like a bodybuilder. His deli is in L.A.

Dad built my deli, Austin Pickle, while I was at the University of Texas.

I rarely visit it. Sure, it's an all-right town. I show up for the big music festivals and drop in whenever a blizzard hits up here. But my little deli does fine without me. Probably better.

Grammy turns from where she's been cooing over

the baby. "Where's Sherman?" she asks, her forehead crinkling in a way that makes us boys stand even straighter.

Max speaks up. "He went to get some balloons."

Grammy nods. She settles in a rocking chair near the bed. "Good to see all you boys in the same place."

"We wouldn't miss it," Anthony says.

A voice booms from the doorway. "It's about time we all got together."

It's Dad, unmistakable in pressed khakis and a freshly ironed button-down. He holds a bouquet of blue balloons so enormous that he must have depleted the stock in the gift store.

"Oh, Uncle Sherman!" Greta exclaims. "That's a lot of balloons!"

He peers around them, his hair a perfect gray wave. "Just want to make sure the newest Pickle knows he's welcome!"

"He's actually a Jones," Jude says from the corner.

"Every Pickle's a Pickle!" Dad insists, and his tone reminds everyone that nobody is to argue with him. He sets the base of the balloon cluster on a side table and approaches us, hand extended. I give him a hefty shake, like he expects.

"Jace," he says. "I hear you tried to make the winning catch."

I sigh. I'm never going to live that down.

He turns to Max. "Now that's a physique. You trying to make your old man look weak?"

Max nods. "You make it too easy, Dad."

Dad mock punches him in the shoulder. "You look good."

When Dad extends a hand to Anthony, he instead pulls Dad into a hug. "Great to see you."

Dad claps him on the back. "You remind me so much of your mother."

Everybody goes quiet. Mom died ten years ago, a loss that never seems to get easier.

"Thank you," Anthony says.

"Saving the old bat for last, are you?" Grammy calls from her corner.

"Always the best for last, Mother." Dad approaches her rocking chair.

I glance over at Max. I still want to kill him.

He gives me a sneer. "How's the playboy mansion?"

"Shut up."

"I saw you went out with that actress. She was terrible in that frat boy movie."

"Shut up."

He laughs. "I'm surprised you graced us with your presence."

"I was already in town."

"Hey," Greta calls from the bed. "Pay attention to the real hero here."

Dad cups the baby's tiny head. "A new Pickle son in the family."

"You going to give him a franchise?" Grammy asks.

"I think the deli business is on your side of the family," Greta says. She gazes down on her son. "Caden can be whoever he wants."

I feel a twinge of jealousy. As the eldest Pickle, I've

been expected to toe the line in the deli business. Sometimes it feels all I've done since leaving home is try to escape it.

Dad clasps his hands behind his back and faces the three of us skulking in the corner. "It seems my own sons don't want to settle down. Why, Greta's the youngest Pickle and here she is, married and providing my brother Martin a grandchild."

"Where are Martin and Fran?" Grammy asks.

"On a flight," Greta answers. "Caden wasn't due for two more weeks."

Dad clears his throat. "We're glad to be here for you, Greta. It's about time my boys started putting family first."

Max's eyebrows draw together in concern. I know what he's thinking.

Lecture incoming.

We think we're saved when a family friend arrives at the door. It's Dell Brant, a New York billionaire who helped Dad find properties to buy as he expanded for us sons. He's like an uncle to us, and his acquisition of an unexpected baby was the talk at our family table a year ago.

But apparently, he's part of whatever Dad's working up to. "Thank you for coming, Dell," Dad says. "I think the boys will have questions for someone as experienced as you when they hear what I have to say."

All three of us glance at each other anxiously. What's going on?

Dad paces in front of where we stand like soldiers lined up for inspection. "When Greta announced she was having a baby, I started thinking about the future. The Pickle franchise is a really big deal."

Chuckles fill the room, since Dad has inadvertently repeated the chain's punny slogan, "A really big *dill*."

He shuts us all up with one steely gaze.

"The delis have sustained my generation, as well as you boys." His eyes meet ours. He gestures to the baby. "And it should help any member of the family who chooses to be a part of it."

"Damn straight," Grammy adds.

Dad nods at her. "But it's time for me to begin the process of stepping down."

Anthony gasps. "Dad! Why?"

"I'm not getting any younger, and I want to make sure the franchise is successful for generations to come."

Grammy speaks up. "Sherman, you're not going to die anytime soon. You're fit as a fiddle."

"That may be, but it's time these boys took over the business. It's getting beyond me anyway, with social media and all. But there's one thing I do know. The company needs a strong leader. One leader." He looks at each of us boys, and we all tense.

Dell nods in agreement. "It's easy for a chain to have conflicting goals if it doesn't remain unified as it transfers from one leader to another."

What are they getting at?

Dad continues. "The three of you have handled the business in different ways, but I wanted to give you all one more opportunity to show me who loves it the most."

"So only one of us can love it the most?" Anthony

asks. He's the soft-hearted brother, so of course he's worried about how we'll all take it.

Dad nods, and visions of not having an income flash in my head. Will all the franchises go to the winning brother? What the hell would I do instead?

But my shoulders relax as Dad says, "Each of you will continue to run the deli you currently possess. However, control of the franchise, including the Manhattan Pickle here in New York, will go to one son."

Max elbows me.

Yeah, I'm the oldest Pickle. I get it. I'm supposed to step up.

I glance at Dell. His eyes are also on me.

Great. This is definitely going to cut into my time at the beach.

But then Dad drops the final bombshell. "The son with the highest profits between this day, March 1st, and the end of the year, will be named the winner."

Anthony, Max, and I glance at each other uneasily. Dad has never pitted us against each other, not when we were small, not when we all picked different sports in adolescence, and certainly not when we began running our own businesses.

Why is he doing it now?

Dad clears his throat. "When you check your email, you'll find our accountant has prepared a financial statement for each deli. Now that you know where you stand compared to the others, you can work on where you want to be by December."

My phone buzzes. I hear a tone from Max's pocket. Then Anthony's.

Dad sure planned this out.

"Anyone who wants to confer with Dell, take this opportunity," Dad says, "He's bought and sold more businesses than I have shirts."

"Think more in the bottles of shampoo range," Dell says, and Dad shakes his head.

Anthony immediately heads toward him, clearly ready to get any advice he can.

My head is still spinning.

Dad gestures to us. "Boys, one of you go pick up some deli trays. I'll call them ahead. Then we'll enjoy this glorious day as a new Pickle has been born healthy and happy."

"I'll do it," I say. I want to look at my email alone. I haven't seen the books on my franchise in months. Maybe over a year.

Okay, maybe never.

It hasn't been an issue. The franchise does fine. It doesn't need me.

But is it enough for me to take over the entire chain? Will it prove I'm the leader of my brothers? Dad almost surely expects me to win. When lectures are handed out, I am usually the target.

I hurry down the hall to the elevator. While I wait, I pull up the email from the accountant.

And read with a terrible, sinking feeling in my stomach.

Even though I own the oldest spin-off franchise and have the most experience, I'm not even close to the other delis in gross, net, or growth.

In every single metric, I'm in the same place.

Dead last.

As I review the figures more closely, I realize it's worse than that.

I'm barely keeping the doors open.

I head down the lobby, realizing my father has thrown down the gauntlet. And I know one thing is true.

Something is terribly wrong with Austin Pickle.

I've *had it* with tiny pickles.

They are straight-up no use to me.

I huff out my annoyance, kicking my heavy boot against the leg of the mixing table. My coworker Lamonte has opened no less than six buckets of the supposedly biggest dill pickles in the United States of America.

I've seen bigger pickles on a dollar store party tray.

And, sometimes, unsolicited in my DMs.

I shove that disgusting thought away as Lamonte plunges his plastic-gloved hands into another drum of pickle juice.

"Nova, I don't think this is the same company we usually get them from."

He's right. The buckets used to be a pale yellow, with the logo of a girl in some old-fashioned costume. These are generic white with the word PICKLES in bold black.

"Do we have the paperwork?" I ask him.

Lamonte withdraws his hands. "I haven't seen papers on a delivery since Susan left. It's all digital."

I stare at his face for a moment. His warm brown eyes are friendly, even though a hint of concern crosses his features. I hired him myself, because our last produce stocker quit without notice, and Susan, Austin Pickle's head manager, has been on extended medical leave for almost six months. In Hawaii.

Nobody believes she's actually sick. Lamonte found her private Instagram, all beach pics and cocktails with umbrellas. She might even still be getting a paycheck. We don't know.

This has left me doing the manager's job on a regular employee's pay. Which I have tried to bring up with our dear boss Jace Pickle a hundred bazillion times. But that man is impossible to get a hold of. He clearly doesn't give one rat's ass about his deli.

It's a good thing I've never met him in person. Because I would probably punch him in the face.

Lamonte arranges the pickles he's salvaged on the cutting board. "Do you think Susan is changing our distributors from her medical leave?"

I shrug. "I sure didn't change it. The supplier chooses the pickles."

It's details like this that make my job harder than it has to be. And without access to the ordering system, which Susan has kept to herself, I can't even double-check anything. For all I know, this deli is one order away from bankruptcy.

Except our lunch rush just ended, and our crew made a hell of a lot of sandwiches.

We take in scads of money every day.

But I still have a pickle problem.

"So, what do we do?" Lamonte asks. "We can't make the stuffed pickles with pickles this small. There's not enough room for the stuffing."

I close my eyes a minute, trying to keep my cool. "I know."

"And we have an order for a hundred stuffed pickles for tomorrow. I have to deliver them at ten a.m."

"I know, Lamonte."

As I keep my vision black for a moment, I contemplate:

> *A. Screaming*
> *B. Throwing pickles*
> *C. Running off to Hawaii on medical leave*
> *D. Shoving pickles up our dear owner's—*

The bell jingles to signal a customer has arrived out front. Lamonte and I are the solitary crew mid-afternoon on a weekday.

"I'll take it," I say. "Keep searching these pickles. If we can't find enough to work with, do what we did last week when the new salami was too salty."

"Grab cash from the register and head to Costco?"

I nod. I hate doing that, because it messes with the books. But technically, I'm not even in charge of the books. And if someone complains about the size of the pickles or the salt in the salami, it's me they come to. Because like it or not, I'm currently the face of Austin Pickle.

I push through the swinging door into the front of the deli.

And almost stop in my tracks. The man who has entered looks like he came straight from a GQ photo shoot.

I can see the headline.

The latest fashion-forward look for the man who has it all.

His pants are fitted like they were sewn directly on his body. I don't know what to call the color. Camel, I guess, or something fancy like *bleached tobacco.*

His shirt is a heathery sort of blue, perfectly pressed and tapered from shoulder to waist. His shoes shine so bright they actually reflect the table legs.

He's out of place in our casual city, but that's not unusual. With our downtown location, we get a lot of visitors. Some of them have come from New York and want to compare our pickle deli with the original in Manhattan.

I make it a matter of personal pride when they tell us ours is just as good, and even better seeing as they didn't have to wait forty-five minutes in line.

Fresh, fast, perfect. Those are the words I keep in my head when I serve something from Austin Pickle.

"Can I help you?"

The man appraises me as he saunters from the door to the counter. "I don't know you," he says.

I plan to be friendly and say something cute like, "Tell me your favorite sandwich, and we'll be best friends."

But the pickle thing has put me in a bad mood.

So instead I say, "You're not from around here."

He takes a step back, an expression I don't expect crossing his face. Concern? Was I too harsh?

I quickly correct myself. "Of course, nobody's a stranger in Austin Pickle for more than a few seconds. Tell me how you take your pickle." I slap on a smile so fake it could win a damn Oscar.

The man relaxes, and the moment passes.

That's good. The last thing I need is a nasty review that gets Jace Pickle all over my case when I'm already struggling to keep his stupid deli going.

Truthfully, I'm counting on a promotion, or at least a good reference for another job. I need to get back to college, and some of the restaurants in town give scholarships to their employees. If this one goes well, I can use it as a leg up somewhere better.

The man leans on the counter. Every strand of his hair is in place, dark and cropped short. The stubble on his chin is perfectly clipped to the precise length to look brooding and sexy. His jaw is sharp enough to break ice.

In fact, the frozen parts of my anatomy are already beginning to thaw.

But he's absolutely not my type. I like my men in jeans and flip-flops, graphic tees for local businesses, well-worn and no fuss.

I bet this guy irons his underwear.

"What did you say your name was?" he asks.

"Nova."

"How long have you worked here?"

Why is he asking this?

"It'll be a year this summer." Last summer I'd run out of money, but stayed in my classes through the Fall semester. I'd only been working part-time, but when Susan took off and most of the employees got worried and quit, I found myself the senior member of the Pickle staff. So, I assumed her responsibilities.

I hadn't thought it would go on this long.

"And your last name?" he asks.

Why does he need my last name? My neck tingles with alarm.

I go for the redirect. "Would you like to sample some of our pickles? We have twelve varieties. We're not the sort of deli that slaps a random spear on the side of your plate. We take pride in the original flavors we produce."

"I'm actually here——" he stops talking when Lamonte emerges from the back room and opens the cash register.

"What's he doing?" the man asks.

"Someone's got to buy the pickles," Lamonte says, lifting a stack of twenties. He fans them out in front of me. "You think this will do it?"

I nod. "Get whatever you need."

Lamonte gives me his signature broad grin and claps me on the back. "I can always count on you. This will totally solve my problem."

He takes off out the front door.

"Did that employee document the money he took from the register?" the man asks.

He sure is pushy about how we run the store.

"It's fine. We found ourselves in a pickle shortage and he's grabbing some more. We do love our pickles around here." I plaster on another fake smile.

The man takes a step back from the counter,

rubbing his hand across his cheek. He seems terribly concerned with what just happened, and visions of another type of online review dance in my head.

"You know," I say. "You look like you could use a sandwich. How about one on the house? Can I recommend the pastrami and rye? It goes wonderfully with our bread and butter jalapeño pickle."

But the man doesn't seem to be paying any attention to me. He circles the room slowly, occasionally touching a chair or gazing at a photo on the wall.

I start to worry he's unhinged. I inch closer to the telephone in case I need to call the police.

"Are you okay?" I call out.

He moves near the door, and I begin to pray he will leave. I don't have time for well-dressed weirdos, no matter how good-looking they are.

And with Lamonte gone, I'm alone until the cleanup crew arrives.

He notices the "Help Wanted" sign in the front window and picks it up.

Good Lord, please tell me he's not here for a job.

I put that sign up yesterday, and two people have filled out applications. Neither one seems very promising, but compared to this crazy guy circling the store, they're starting to look good.

The man turns around. "Who does the hiring for the store?"

Oh, no. I knew it.

"Well, normally it would be our general manager Susan." I hesitate, not wanting to give this lunatic her last name either.

"But…"

"She's on medical leave."

"So who is interviewing the people who come in to apply?"

I do *not* want to tell him that it's me. Maybe I should pawn it off on the owner. Yes. That's exactly what I'll do. It'll serve Jace Pickle right for never being around. He can deal with this crazy man.

"You can contact the owner," I suggest. "His name is Jace Pickle."

Shoot, he's walking back to the counter. I lay my hand on top of the phone. One wrong move, buster, and I'm picking this sucker up.

"You haven't had any new hires since the manager left?"

I falter. "Well, sure, but…"

"That other fellow seemed to act like you were in charge."

"Well, I have been, since Susan's been out."

He stares me down. Who is this guy? We once had a couple of men arrive who insisted on speaking to the Pickles because they wanted to buy this building. But they hadn't been as adamant and scary as this one.

"What position is open?" he asks.

"Just an all-around helper. Start on chopping and work up to the sandwich line."

When he frowns, I think I'm scot-free. Mr. GQ isn't going to want to slap mustard on bread. Feeling bolder, I say, "And yes, I'm able to hire for that. But it's clearly not your type of work."

And just like that, something in him changes. He

taps the sign against his hand. He looks around the restaurant once again. Then he comes back to me. "Do you know Jace Pickle?"

"I know he's the owner. I've never met him."

He sets the sign on the top of the counter. "Well, I do. And he assured me I could get a job at this deli."

"What? You?"

He holds out his arms. "I can get my hands dirty like anyone else."

I'm flabbergasted. "Your outfit costs more than you will make in a week."

"I just finished my degree and want to run a restaurant chain myself," he says smoothly. He's completely turned his personality around, flashing me a charming smile. "Jace kindly offered me a position here so I could learn the ropes. He talks very highly about how this restaurant is managed. He may have even mentioned you by name. Nova, right?"

I'm not moved. This man is slicker than snake oil now. Besides, I already told him my name. "I have to talk to Jace Pickle about this."

"Absolutely. You do that," he says. "Just tell him Jason arrived to start the job."

"Do you have a last name?"

"He'll know who Jason is," he says. "We're best buds. Just call. Trust me."

"I never get a hold of him when I try. He's apparently very busy."

This Jason person frowns at that. "I'll mention it to him. I know he's a hands-off guy. It's because he trusts you so much. I'm sorry I made a bad impression. I was just so surprised to see the place empty. I got the impression this was a very successful store."

"It's mid-afternoon on a Tuesday," I say, leaving the chill in my voice. "You should've been here an hour ago. The line was out the door."

He nods. "Good, great. Sounds like you could use my help for lunches. You give him a call this afternoon and tell him I'll be here tomorrow morning to assist with the lunch rush. Or to chop things? Isn't that what you said the job was?"

Who is this guy? He would probably come in here with his MBA or whatever and try to make us do whatever he learned in business class. Hire focus groups. Or something worse. Like hold *meetings*.

Hopefully, I won't be able to get a hold of Jace, and I can send this guy packing. I really will call the police.

"Just leave your number," I say. "If I get the go-ahead from Mr. Pickle, then I'll let you know what time to be here."

He grabs a napkin and scribbles the digits. "That sounds perfect. I'm excited to be joining this team."

With that, he takes off out of the store and into the bright March afternoon.

Holy crap.

What was that?

I'm hesitant to even call Jace Pickle about this. He'll probably laugh at me for being so gullible as to think the owner would send some random man-model to work on the sandwich line.

The whole thing seems off.

But what if he *is* a friend? I need this job to go well.

I have a whole future ahead of me, or at least I think I do.

Probably it doesn't matter. I'll never talk to Jace Pickle. It hasn't worked all the times I've tried since Susan left. And she mentioned back in the day that he was extremely difficult to reach. Sometimes she called Anthony, the Pickle brother who owns the Colorado branch, for clarifications. He, apparently, is great.

Maybe I should be working for *that* Pickle.

Still, I guess I have to try.

I flip through the directory in the drawer below the counter until I find Jace Pickle's personal number. As soon as I see the digits, I frown and turn around the napkin Jason handed me.

They have the same area code. In the era of cell phones, this doesn't always matter, but it did suggest Jason's story isn't as far-fetched as it seemed.

Maybe they grew up together. Maybe his family put him up to it. Shoot. I have a sinking feeling this particular story might be true.

I quickly dial Jace's number.

Instead of rolling to voicemail, the call connects with a female voice.

"Office of Jace Pickle, can I help you?"

Since when did he have a secretary on his personal line?

"I need to speak with Mr. Pickle. I'm Nova Strong. I work at his deli."

"Oh, hello, Nova. Jace said to expect your call. Did Jason make it into the deli? We're hoping you have space for him there."

Well, shoot. It's true.

This can't be some elaborate scheme if I called *him*. This directory has been here since I got the job.

"Should I talk to Mr. Pickle himself?"

"He's away at the moment. We don't think Jason will bother you for very long. He's not the sort of guy who gets his hands dirty for more than a few days." Her laugh is like glass tinkling. "Make him do everything all the regular employees do. He's not to get special treatment."

That's promising, at least. "Do I have him fill out all the paperwork? And give him the usual starting hourly wage?"

"You know, I'm not sure about that part. Have him fill out the forms, but before you cut any checks, I'll get you an answer. Probably he's going to be happy to work for free. But I'll make sure."

"Okay, thanks."

I set down the phone, feeling aghast.

I have a new employee.

Hot. Smart. Well-dressed.

Able to turn on the charm when necessary.

Stupidly good-looking.

And he has to do what I say. *Everything* I say.

No special treatment.

He might be wealthy or well educated or well-born.

But now, I'm his *boss*.

3

JACE

The moment I walk out the door of Austin Pickle, I call my personal assistant, Audra, to tell her I'm forwarding my personal number to her, and to instruct Nova Strong when she calls that, yes, Jason is supposed to start working there tomorrow.

I can give no more information than that before ending the connection and temporarily forwarding my calls to her.

Now I have to wait to see how it goes. Audra is smart and thinks on her feet. She'll handle everything well.

I relax against the leather seats of the BMW I keep in Austin for my visits. I'm sitting at the far end of a parking lot with a direct view of Austin Pickle. I can't clearly see inside the deli, but since it's currently empty, I know any movement is almost certainly Nova.

Nova Strong.

I sure didn't expect her. Tiny as a mite. Sparkling brown eyes. More personality than a Saturday morning cartoon. And apparently, running the place.

I hadn't had a plan when I stormed through the door, and I know I annoyed her. And I nearly blew my stack when that employee took money out of the till. Straight out! No receipts, nothing!

And he's off to buy pickles? From where? Wal-mart? There's no way they can be up to the Pickle franchise standard.

No wonder my branch is in such a tailspin. No manager. This spitfire hiring whomever she likes. Sourcing product from who knows where.

Thank God for the help wanted sign. It gave me this perfectly terrible but brilliant idea to get inside the operation. Figure out where everything's gone wrong.

Then I can fire everybody involved.

Including Nova and her cash-pilfering employee.

Something buzzes in my console. It can't be my phone since my calls and texts are forwarded. God, I hope nobody sends a naughty text to me while Audra's in control. I don't have a current flame, but there are plenty of potentials I've pursued recently.

Audra's a professional, but she has a wicked sense of humor. She'll kid me about it forever.

I open the lid. I have an iPad in there, the small version. It's the source of the buzz. The number to call it is the one I gave Nova. Has she already contacted me?

But it's a message from Audra.

Call complete. Jason is a go. You can un-forward your calls. Oh, and Shania sent a lovely picture of her new nipple ring.

What! I haven't seen that woman in ages!

Shit!

Then another message.

Just kidding. But you bought it, didn't you?

Oh, that Audra.

I write her back.

Ha, ha. And thanks.

I remove the forward.

Nova was fast. But I was faster.

I sit there a little longer, watching a mother with two small children enter my deli. I hope Nova gives them better customer service than she did me. Even if I had been a bit of an ass.

But everything is upside down in there. How long has my manager been gone?

And who is managing the books? The orders? The deliveries?

I have no idea. No wonder I'm dead last in the race for best deli.

I lean back against the headrest and thread my fingers together.

This seems like a lot of work. Maybe I shouldn't even bother.

Everybody knows Anthony's deli is managed the best, and he cares the most. I could let him win and be done with it

But when I peer across the parking lot at the front awning of Austin Pickle, I know I can't do that. It's not the Pickle way. Dad raised us to do our best, to be competitive, to win. And the fact is, I'm not sure I like this impression that his eldest son has learned nothing from his old man. That I don't care about the legacy he started.

So no, I'm not going to throw the challenge. I'm

going to get in there tomorrow and learn how to make my own damn sandwiches. Figure out how many nonstandard financial procedures are going down. And ultimately, get rid of any bad apples on my staff, including this Nova Strong person if need be.

And who knows. Maybe I will turn out to be such a terrific boss and entrepreneur that I'll actually win this thing.

The next morning, I arrive at Austin Pickle at nine sharp. The text from Nova with my reporting time came through a couple of hours after my conversation with Audra.

She's reliable at least.

I park my BMW in a garage a few blocks down to avoid attention. Nova has already accused me of being too uppity for sandwich work.

I've tried to mimic the way the other employee dressed. Faded jeans. T-shirt. Didn't we have Pickle shirts for the employees? Dad did in Manhattan. I've never visited my brothers' delis in Boulder and L.A.

Should we? Maybe not. It's another expense when I'm trying to squeeze out some profit.

The door is locked when I approach. Right. We don't open until eleven.

The deli is part of a block of buildings. There's no easy way to get around to a back door.

My iPad is in the car, and I can't call or text on my personal phone or I'll blow my cover.

Great start, Jace. Great start.

I peer through the glass. Nova is in there, along with the employee from yesterday and two women. They're all busy taking chairs down and filling napkin dispensers and messing with the tea machines.

I watch Nova for a moment. She laughs easily with her crew, climbing up on the cabinet to peer in the top of the soda dispenser. She fixes something and jumps down, her brown hair flying behind her.

I'm momentarily distracted by the way her breasts bounce when suddenly the door opens. I stumble forward.

"Jason, I assume?" It's the man from yesterday, tall and lean with a smirking grin. He holds out an arm to make sure I don't fall.

I straighten up. "Yeah, that's me."

Nova turns. "Oh, hey, Jason." She glances at my outfit. "I see you came dressed for work today."

I nod, tugging at the cotton shirt uncomfortably. I'd picked it up at a local record shop. It reads "Keep Austin Weird."

"Killer jeans, though," the man says. "They must have set you back."

Maybe I should have downgraded my Fendi to Gap or something.

"I'm Lamonte." The man extends a hand. "Welcome to Austin Pickle."

I grasp it firmly. "Jason."

He grins like I'm an idiot. Right. He already said my name.

He releases me and points at a young woman with a

blond ponytail. "That's Kate. She goes to UT." Then he gestures to a middle-aged Hispanic woman. "And that's Elda."

I give them both a wave.

"What should I do first?" I'll toe the line for a bit, but as soon as I get a chance, I plan to get into the manager's office and review the books.

"I think Nova's got some paperwork."

Right. I should probably get out of that. No use complicating things. I wish I'd been able to have Audra communicate this, but we'd been short on time to talk about details before Nova called. I head to the counter.

Nova pushes a couple of sheets of paper my way. "Most of this is just a formality. Job application, even though you've already got the job. And the tax paperwork."

"Oh, I don't need to fill any of that out," I say.

Nova's smile goes forced. "I'm afraid you do. Jace Pickle's instructions from his assistant specifically said you were to fill out the forms, and she'd get back to me on the pay scale. And also, *no special treatment*."

She seems to relish saying it. My suspicions about her rise another notch. Is she trying to get me out of here? Does she have something to hide, and she's afraid I'll find it?

"Fine," I say, turning the paper around.

I scratch out the information, using my Manhattan address, which isn't connected to any of the other Pickles, and the iPad phone number.

Then I drop my pen. "Done. Should I head to the back? Scrub up?"

"In a sec." Nova Strong examines my job application like a calculus teacher needing someone to flunk. "What do you know about deli work?" Her voice is practically a bark. The woman must have been a drill sergeant in a former life. Or maybe this one, judging by the camo pants and Army boots.

Still, the soft black tank top hugs her curves, softening the effect of the bottom half of her outfit. She's a pistol, no doubt about it.

"I've made a sandwich or two," I say.

She sighs, blowing a puff of hair off her forehead. She's as gorgeous as she is fierce. It's a combination that's increasingly setting me off balance, even though I suspect she's up to no good.

I attempt a grateful expression, which, admittedly, is not my forte. "I appreciate the opportunity."

She stabs the application. "I'm going to need some ID to prove this really is your name."

My jaw tightens. Dad insisted we all live publicly as Pickles to support the franchise name. But in reality, we jumped at the chance. Because in our business, our birth name is incredibly, most horribly worse.

I pull out my wallet to hand her my ID. Thankfully it lists the matching address.

Nova can't fight back her grin. "How do you pronounce that, Jason?"

I sigh. "Just like it's spelled."

"I want to be sure I'm getting it right."

I glance around the room. The other employees are listening in, even though they act like they're working.

I lean in.

"It's Packwood."

Giggles erupt from the college students. I glance at Lamonte, who is working hard to keep his face straight. Elda has her back to us.

Nova's expression is poker serious. "Packwood. I haven't heard that name before."

"It's not that rare. And you have my ID right there."

She shakes her head. "I guess I wouldn't know how to spot a fake ID from New York."

What? She doesn't believe me?

"Immigrants were named by what they did."

"And your people pack *wood*?"

Now Lamonte has lost it. He's bent over, mouth covered. Kate has dashed to the back, lost in giggles. Elda still faces away, but her shoulders are shaking.

I try to find my inner Zen.

Nova's expression is stern, but her eyes sparkle with mischief. "It's a great name. I can't wait to put it on an employee pin."

Her curvy little tank—and I admit I linger on it longer than I should—doesn't sport a pin.

"Where's yours?"

"Oh, we haven't had them made in a while," she says. "Turnover was so high it didn't make sense."

"But now..."

"Oh yes. I think we definitely need to bring them back." She clips the pages together. "I'll put these away. There are aprons in the back. We'll get you started on the cutting board."

She calls out, "Lamonte, can you show Jason where the knives are? And make sure he can handle himself.

We don't want his blood in the potato salad." She glares at me. "You can head on back."

I find Lamonte by a long stainless-steel table in the center of the room and accept the apron he hands me. Hopefully, I can focus on the work and not that difficult woman.

I'm trying to have a sense of humor about this, but my deli is proving to have too little pickle, and too much brine.

4

NOVA

Jason Packwood strikes me as a pain in the ass, but at least he seems to have a work ethic. I check in on him and Lamonte chopping vegetables in the kitchen before prepping the line to serve.

Elda has the drink station all set up. Kate is getting the tables in order. I make sure the hot and cold temperatures are all set appropriately and began placing the vats of meats and cheeses in their slots along the counter.

Lamonte will have to leave shortly to deliver the stuffed pickle order he prepped early this morning. I punch in a receipt and open the fridge that holds all the pickup and delivery orders.

We don't do as much of these as we used to, and I wonder if this is something the old manager did well, a facet of the business that is suffering in her absence. Now that I have a corporate spy of sorts with this Jason guy, who undoubtedly will report anything weird straight to his dear friend Jace Pickle, I should try again to get the passwords to turn on the main computer in Susan's office.

I feel so in the dark about everything. It's all I can do to keep the store going, and pray we always get sufficient deliveries and the bills are somehow paid. Last week the distributor of the specialty peppers insisted we cut a check on the spot. I simply had to take the old check-book—which we rarely used since Susan would print the official ones on her computer—and scribble out the amount on his invoice. It was either that or not have three of our signature dishes.

Of course, yesterday we had the tiny pickle dilemma.

I might be low on crew at the moment, but the ones I do have are reliable. Still, Kate will leave at the end of May, when she heads home for the summer. She's why I already put out a notice for a new employee, hoping to get someone trained before I lose her.

Lamonte pushes through the swinging door. "I'm headed out to deliver those pickles."

"Do you think you'll make it back before the rush?" I ask.

"Should." He leans in closer. "I'm a little short on gas money, though. Payday's not till tomorrow."

I nod. Lamonte is perpetually short on gas money. We worked out a system where I sometimes front him part of his paycheck, and as soon as he cashes it, he returns the money to the till.

It's never once been a problem. But by the time I put in the code to open the register, Jason has stuck his head through the door to watch.

Spying.

I had a feeling. I slam the register closed without removing any money. "Take my car. The keys are in my cubbie."

I shouldn't feel an ounce of guilt as I turn to Jason, but I somehow do. Even though I've done absolutely nothing wrong, not today or yesterday, with the cash register, I feel a twinge. I keep track of any money coming out of the register on a sticky note underneath the tray. But it *is* an irregularity. There's no electronic trail, and no one checks my work or approves what I do.

"Did you finish the onions?" I ask Jason.

Jason wipes his eye with the back of his wrist, since his hands are covered in plastic gloves. "I was going to ask Lamonte if I chopped them fine enough."

Lamonte shuts the fridge with his shoulder, an insulated delivery bag in each hand. "Nova, can you check? He could use some tips. His dicing skills need work. He can't mince."

I glance at the sandwich line to see what still needs to be done. "Elda, can you put out the pickles? I'm headed to the back."

Jason pushes the door open for me to pass through. I catch a strong whiff of onions and jalapeños as I walk by. Lamonte gave him the worst cutting assignments.

But beneath that, I catch a trace of something woodsy and expensive. Aftershave? Probably not. He still sports the same scruffy, tumbled-out-of-bed look he had yesterday.

Cologne, I guess. I've never been around a cologne

guy. It seems fussy. None of my other male friends are fussy. Not by a longshot.

Even though he's dressed down for the occasion, Jason still holds the appearance of someone distinctly upper-class. I don't know enough to put my finger on what it might be. The stitching on his jeans? The perfect way they hug his hips? The fit of the T-shirt, obviously new, tucked casually into the front band of his jeans, but not in the back?

I've seen that before. I watch *Queer Eye*. It's a French tuck. I'm not sure who does that on a daily basis, but certainly not anyone I know.

At least, not until now.

We head to the counter where he's been chopping onions.

It's a travesty. I grab a glove and slide it on. "Well, this leaves a lot to be desired." I lift a handful in my palm like an accusation. "There are no less than five distinct sizes in these onions."

"Lamonte tried to show me, but I think it's going to take some practice," Jason says.

I drop the onions to the cutting board. "We can't have someone taking a bite of our classic chicken salad, which is where these particular onions are headed, and suddenly get a big honking bite of raw onion. The flavors have to blend precisely the right way."

For a moment, Jason watches me curiously. "You care about how things taste, don't you?"

"Of course I do. It's Austin Pickle. We have a reputation to uphold!"

"It's pickles!"

"It's our twelve special kinds of pickles."

I grab a spare knife and slice through the onions, rapidly mincing them to the fine bits necessary to make chicken salad work.

I move down to the jalapeños. "Lamonte didn't show you anything? These are supposed to be super thin. The jalapeños are really potent."

"I tried to do what he was doing." Jason sounds genuinely frustrated.

"I can't use these. We don't serve anything with chopped jalapeños, and the slices are way too thick." I slide the entire set off the cutting board and into the compost at the end. "Show me how you're holding the knife."

Jason lifts his knife parallel to the board. I pass him a fresh jalapeño.

He slices it down the middle and scrapes out the seeds.

"So far, so good," I say.

He turns the jalapeño flat side down and lifts the knife.

I immediately say, "Stop!"

He freezes his slice mid-air. "What?"

"The knife should not be in the air. Keep the tip on the cutting board and bring it down like it's one of those old-fashioned paper cutters from school."

"I remember those. My friend dared me to see if it would cut off my finger."

"And were you stupid enough to try?" I cock my hip, arms crossed. Surely, he isn't that dumb.

"I was an eight-year-old boy! Of course I tried it."

I feel a laugh bubbling up inside me, but I squelch it down. "So how many stitches did you require?"

"Three. But it was worth it."

Now I do have to laugh. "What made it worth it?"

"Every girl in the class brought me cookies and cards."

That sobers me up. "So, you were a playboy even then?"

His grin is slow and easy, and I'm reminded of when he turned on the charm yesterday after deciding he needed to switch tactics with me.

I go on alert. Snake oil. He's laying it on thick now.

"Who says I'm a playboy?"

I shrug. "I can spot them. I meet a ton of them at UT."

He sets down his knife. "You go to UT?"

Heat rises from my neck. I really don't want to go into this with him. "I did."

"You graduated but you work here?"

I don't know if it's real confusion or pity, but I don't like it.

"I haven't finished yet," I snap. "Let's see if you can cut a jalapeño worthy of serving on our sandwich line or if you're a complete waste of space."

He's not bothered by my insult. His perfect eyebrows move together in concern. Hating him would be a whole lot easier if he wasn't so pretty.

"I get it. You don't talk about it." He turns back to the jalapeño. He leans down very close to the green pepper. "All right, my friend. I am very sorry I have to cut you into pieces. But apparently, my unpaid position is on the line. So help me out and I'll be merciful."

All right, I have to admit it. He's funny. My shoulders relax. "Just get on with it," I say, but my tone doesn't have the bite like before.

He grins at me, and my belly flips. *Stop it, traitorous stomach.*

"So, I keep the tip on the counter and then I bring it down." He slices the first cut.

"Perfect. Curl your left hand so you're not putting your fingers in the line of fire. I won't be bringing you cards and cookies if you need stitches."

He grins at me again. "You sure?"

"Positive. Make a claw."

"Like this?" He rolls back his fingers.

"Yeah. And push the pepper with your thumb."

He still doesn't have it, so I pick up another knife and show him the motion.

"All right," he says, but he still lifts his knife in the air.

I put my hand over his wrist. "Like this," I say. "Tip down, rocking motion."

We slice the pepper together. Our hands are covered in plastic, but our arms are bare. My skin brushes against his, and the touch is electric. I quickly step away.

"Did I do something wrong?" he asks.

"No. I think you've got it. Those slices are good. Carry on."

I back out of the kitchen as quickly as possible, bumping into a rolling cart as I go.

He doesn't remark on that but continues his slow methodical slices.

As I whirl around and blow through the door to the front of the deli, my face flames.

What the hell was that?

A spark? A silly, ridiculous spark? A romance novel, sappy Hallmark movie, gross cliché spark?

I rip off the gloves and rub my arm as if it'd been burned.

I've had boyfriends before. I know what it's like to be interested in someone.

It's nothing like what just happened.

Those guys were normal. They wore regular clothes. Had average jobs. Real problems. They didn't demand positions at deli counters while wearing designer clothes.

And they didn't talk to jalapeños.

That was a *hate spark*. Or static electricity.

Or maybe a warning shot from the universe to stay away from that guy.

But I know for sure it's definitely not what it seems.

It is *not* a spark of attraction.

5

JACE

On a normal evening, I hit my peak around ten p.m. Usually, I've had a lovely dinner somewhere, often with delightful company.

We'll have stopped at a local watering hole to have a drink while discussing where to spend the bulk of the night. Around that magical hour, we've made our decision and I'm closing the tab so we can travel to our new destination. We're full of anticipation, ready to mingle and be part of a scene.

Everywhere I normally live, there's all manner of clubs and music venues and upscale bars. We can dance. Or talk. Or watch dancers. Or even take in some culture. Often, though, we're ushered into private lounges with high-end clientele. Interesting people who've made a killing on Wall Street or had directorial debuts or financed a new Broadway play.

But not here.

Not this night.

After my first day working in my own deli, I startle

awake on the sofa of my downtown condo and realize I've fallen asleep in my clothes.

I lift my T-shirt to my nose and wince. It smells of pickle juice and raw onion.

The tips of my fingers are all nicked from what had to be twenty thousand tomatoes, cucumbers, and other vegetables I sliced and diced.

And julienned. Why did carrots have to be chopped into tiny sticks? Weren't there machines for that? I have to ask Anthony about this. It seems like a ridiculous use of labor.

Especially *my* labor.

It's ten p.m. and I'm officially a snoozer.

At least there's no one around to see. I run my hands through my hair and shake off the fuzz on my brain. It's the height of the evening in Austin, Texas, and I've become a boring old man.

I drop my feet to the floor and realize I have one shoe on and one shoe off. Really? I fell asleep in the middle of taking off my shoes?

And what are those spots on the top of my two-thousand-dollar Berlutis?

Grease. Great.

I need to call my personal shopper and get something more suitable. What time is it in New York?

Eleven. I shouldn't call her this late.

Tomorrow I can wear my workout shoes. Most everyone else wore some variation of sneaker. I should have thought of it today.

I rub my eyes with the back of my hands and feel the sting of jalapeño juice. I swear I scrubbed them half a dozen times. It's like it's embedded in my skin, and I'm sweating it out.

I don't know how many sandwiches we made. I don't know how many customers we served. I don't see any reason why my deli is doing as badly as it is on paper. Not with the crowd that went through.

Something is terribly wrong.

I shuffle to the bathroom to shower and scrub off every last trace of the smell from the sandwich line.

All this and I still don't have any new information. Other than it looked like Nova and Lamonte were about to take money out of the cash register a second time. Gas money. How much gas money has he pilfered from the till? Enough to affect my bottom line?

How do I even account for that? How would I know it was gone if they were taking cash sales? Only credit cards went through the accounting office, and the staff could easily do cash transactions without putting them through the system. Who did the books for the branch? Made cash deposits? Had there even been any? Was all the cash disappearing?

I turn on the faucet and splash my face. I don't even know what I don't know. Sure, I toured my own deli when it first opened. And I visit it every now and then, giving the staff a quick pep talk before showing myself out.

Dad used the template of his business to start mine. As far as I know, Max's L.A. Pickle and Anthony's Boulder Pickle are the same. I'll ask them about the books, the software, the checks and balances.

Except they're the competition.

Plus, they'll laugh me into next week.

And about Nova. Why did she appoint herself in charge of the store? And how come I hadn't heard my manager took off? What was she doing anyway? Lamonte had joked about her medical leave in Hawaii. And I admit it sounds a little ludicrous.

I'll have Audra check into that.

Maybe the accountant knows something. He manages the whole chain's payroll and taxes. I'll put Audra on that too.

Meanwhile, I have to keep working while I watch for any other irregularities. Nobody went into the manager's office while I was on shift.

I have the keys. And the passwords to everything. My administrative access is higher than the manager's. That was one thing I made sure I could do before I flew down here. Our centralized tech company assured me there would be no problem getting access to the computer files. All orders, deliveries, invoicing, and expense sheets would be mine.

And tomorrow, I will do just that.

If Nova gives me a moment's break to do so.

Day two in Pickle Hell turns out to be Lamonte's day off. In his place is another youngish fellow named Arush. He prepares a great vat of chicken salad. Apparently, he's aces at it.

Nova sends me back to the chopping block with new bins of vegetables, and I get started.

This day is harder, the cuts on my fingers slowing me down. But Nova watches me for a moment, nods in satisfaction at the size and consistency of my dicing and takes off.

I keep chopping for a while, listening to the rest of the staff chat as they set up the restaurant for the day. Clearly, the low man in the hierarchy gets to do the vegetables alone.

Arush leaves to fill the bins in the sandwich line.

It's time to snoop.

I set down my knife and tiptoe toward the swinging door. A single round window provides a view of the front.

Nova and Elda busily arrange the sandwich line, working around Arush. I should have a few moments to slip into the office and see what I can find.

I pull the key from my pocket and hurry to the back corner.

The manager's office is a small space built near the delivery door. It's fairly private. Only a small square window for looking out into the workspace, and another one on the back wall gives a view of the parking lot where the delivery trucks pull up.

As soon as I step inside, I grab several pieces of paper from the printer to cover the little window so no one can see in.

When I've got it taped up, I snap on the light.

The office is dusty, as if it hasn't been used in some time. The desk is shoved into one corner, shelves on the wall above it lined with black binders stuffed with paper.

The desk itself is mostly clear, a calendar propped

up against the back wall. The dates are for last fall. No one has torn off a sheet in six months.

The computer monitor rests angled in a corner, and I reach down to power on the PC. While it whines into startup mode, I pull down one of the binders from above.

It's filled with order receipts from two years ago. I shove it back up. I open each one until I find the most recent. They stop about the same time as the calendar with a note that the ordering system has gone electronic.

Good. Computer files are easier to search and compare.

I open the drawer directly in front of the chair. Nothing but pens and random office supplies.

I don't expect anything obvious. In fact, I don't have a clue about what I'm looking for. It's not like I'll find a secret file folder labeled *Embezzled Funds.*

But I do run my hand underneath the bottom of the desk just in case.

The screen glows blue and prompts me to enter a password.

I pull out my phone to open the email from my tech guy. He gave me the back-end method of opening the computer.

I tap on a nearly invisible icon in the corner, and yet another password prompt pops up. I enter what I was given, and the computer shifts to a screen full of icons for applications.

Now we're getting somewhere.

I've just found a folder marked *Accounting* when a

whoosh of air proceeds the slam of the door against the wall.

I have company.

"What the hell are you doing in here?"

I don't have to look to know it's Nova. Definitely pissed off.

I spin around in the chair.

"Trying to learn all aspects of the business so I can run my own," I lie smoothly.

"I call bullshit." Nova's cheeks burn red, and interestingly enough, so does what cleavage I can see in today's tank top.

It's dark green, and my eyes linger before returning to her blazing face.

"Explain yourself before I throw your ass out on the street."

I hold up my hands in innocence. "It's like I said. Jace told me there's a certain accounting software they use, and I should get familiar with it."

"Bullshit!" Nova snarls. "Accounting software is business school 101."

I gesture to the screen. "Why don't you show me? I could use your expertise."

"How did you even get in here?" Nova asks. "I have the only extra key. Susan took hers."

I open my mouth, but I can't come up with a clever answer fast enough for Nova.

"You know what," she says, "that's it. You're out. Jace Pickle can shove his pompous rich protégé right up his ass."

I jump up. "I'll go back to my cutting. I will. I thought I could look——"

"No. I won't have this. Sneaking around, not even knowing what you're up to. You could be some corporate spy. How well does Jace even know you?" She jerks off her plastic gloves in frustration. "No. Until I talk to Jace Pickle myself, and I am cleared of any responsibility of whatever havoc you could wreak by breaking into the manager's office, I need you off this property."

Damn, she's a spitfire. Just watching her eyes flash sends my groin tightening. Nobody I date would ever act like this.

"This isn't necessary. Just give Jace a call."

"Oh, I will," she says. "But you won't be here when I do it. Leave."

"Nova, calm down." I take a step toward her, giving her my best pleading expression.

"Do *not* tell me to calm down. Who actually calms down when someone tells them to calm down? Get off this property before I call the police."

She's damn beautiful when she's mad. The blush of her skin has spread across her shoulders. So, this was what Nova Strong looks like when she's full of fire. I wonder if it's the same in the throes of passion.

Her eyes blaze, and the cute ponytail hairstyle is an adorable foil to her expression. I fight an overwhelming urge to kiss her.

"I'm calling the police," she hisses and jerks her cell phone from her pocket.

"You sure you want to do that? I'm tight with the boss."

"I am absolutely fucking sure." She practically beams lasers at me.

I can handle the police, but my cover will be blown. I'll have to manage this myself. Or, I guess, have Audra do it.

I pull my white apron over my head and hand it to her.

She watches my every move as I walk out of the office and through the kitchen.

The moment I'm outside, I call my assistant.

Her voice holds a laugh. "Did she fire you already?"

"How did you know?"

"I was expecting that call yesterday."

"Well, she kicked me out for turning on the manager's computer. Can you talk to her?"

"What do you want me to say?"

"Just back me up that Jace wants Jason to learn the software. It shouldn't be that hard."

"All right, Jace. But you know how this is going to end, right?"

I run my hand through my hair, distinctly aware I reek of onions as I pass through the professional crowd maneuvering the downtown sidewalks. "How?"

"With you cold busted and your brothers bringing this up every holiday."

"I'll have to risk it."

"All right. Forward your phone. I'll do what I can."

I sigh in relief. "You're a peach. Should I give you a raise?"

"I gave myself one in December. And a Christmas bonus."

"You deserve it."

"Now forward the phone before she calls."

I hang up and forward the number.

I plunk down on a bench a couple of blocks down from the deli, the green-and-white-striped awning barely visible.

I am the biggest loser in the family.

My store is failing.

And Nova Strong just kicked me out of my own damn deli.

How the hell did I get here?

6

NOVA

H ow the hell did Jason Packwood get here?

Who sent him?

Who is that man, really?

I stand at the glass door of the deli, making sure this Jason jerk-off walks away.

I did not sign up for this.

Not the manager position. Not even working full-time.

Certainly not having a corporate spy nosing around the manager's office.

I have enough problems trying to keep this place going. The last thing I need is some snoopy stranger.

When Jason is safely down the block, I lock the front door and head to the kitchen. Arush and Elda have the sandwich line preparation well in hand. Eli will be here shortly, and I will put him on chopping.

I walk back into Susan's office. I haven't been here in a few weeks, not since I had to manually write that check. I was lucky to convince the cleaning staff to give me the extra key to this room. But, since I have it, they don't come in here anymore. There's a coat of dust on everything.

Because of this, I can tell everywhere Jason snooped. He covered the window, obviously wanting to hide what he was doing.

He took some binders down.

And powered up the computer.

But look at this.

He's in.

I haven't been able to log-on in six months. Susan doesn't respond to emails or phone calls. I had no way of getting the password.

But this Jason guy was able to.

For a moment, my stomach quivers. Was I wrong? Rash?

It wouldn't be the first time. I'm not exactly known for my calm, steady demeanor.

Still, this is an opportunity.

Before I was elevated to the position of acting manager, brought upon by no one else being willing to do the job, and our infuriating owner leaving us to our own devices, I had only glanced at the screen a time or two while Susan entered data.

But I have a degree in business—well, half of one anyway—and our classes reviewed the different types of software that's out there.

I recognize this one. It's nothing original or privately developed. I double-click on the accounting folder and find all the files and backups dating to when Susan left. Maybe now I can review all the vendors to see where things have changed and figure out why. All I have to do is make sure this machine doesn't power down again and force a new login.

Or. Hmm.

What level of access does it have right now? I click through and realize, yes, this is administrative level. I quickly go and create a new user, title it *Acting Manager*, and give it a new login and password. This should bypass Susan.

I copy all the files into this profile for safekeeping and hide them in a folder titled *Old Redundant Backups* so no one will care about it.

I don't have time to go through things right now. I'm less than an hour away from when we open.

But I'm in.

Before I go, I change the computer settings to never shut down. This will ensure it doesn't restart with unexpected security. As long as there isn't a power outage, and nobody manually powers it down or unplugs it, I'll have plenty of time after we close to go through the files.

And I won't have nosy old Jason looking over my shoulder.

In fact, maybe I won't call Jace Pickle. That guy is gone, and now that he's out the door, I don't have to worry about corporate spies.

Or *hate sparks*.

The deli has only been closed for maybe fifteen minutes when Elda approaches me in the industrial freezer.

"Phone call for you," she says. She glances around the outrageously stuffed freezer shelves. "Dios mio!"

"I know," I say. Everything on the sandwich line is fresh, but the specialized desserts we serve come frozen. Cheesecakes. Chocolate tortes. A whole line of sweets that never seem to appeal to our lunch crowd.

I'd like to cancel the automatic shipment but talking to the man who brings them has been useless, since he's just a delivery guy. So they stack up. Maybe I can run a dessert special in hopes of clearing them out. Free cheesecake with a sandwich or something.

I turn to Elda. "Did they say who they were?"

"I didn't ask," Elda says. "I'm not a secretary."

"It's fine. I'll get it." I follow Elda out of the freezer and shut the door. Kate handles our calls when she's here, taking telephone orders and managing all the salespeople. She's good at it. I'm always tempted to slam the phone down when someone gets pushy.

Since the manager's office is already open, I step inside and take the call at Susan's old desk.

"Austin Pickle. This is Nova. Can I help you?"

"Hi. This is Audra, Jace Pickle's assistant."

Her again. Her melodious voice sets me on edge. She sounds perfect. She probably wears some trendy business suit with a clever scarf and four-inch heels that don't trip her every third step.

"Yeah?" I don't hide my annoyance at her call.

She almost laughs. "I understand Jason caused a problem for you today."

"I caught him snooping. If Jace Pickle wants to spy on his own deli, he can do it himself. He shouldn't send a stooge. And if Jason wasn't authorized to be combing through the manager's computer, then you should be glad I kicked him out."

Now this woman's laugh is full-throated. "I heard you were something else."

My jaw clamps tight. What does that mean?

Audra goes on. "Look, personally, I think Jason is a big pain in the ass. I think he should go back to his playpen with his rich little friends and stop trying to act like he cares about running a business. He's about as suited for it as a monkey in a pile of manure."

Okay, that gets a laugh out of me. Maybe I like this woman.

"So, what do we do?"

"I spoke with Jace about it, but he is adamant we let Jason fail."

Seriously? I grip the phone tightly. "So we're trying to teach this boneheaded rich kid a lesson. And I have to be the one who takes it? No. I'm not going to do that."

"I'm with you, but—"

"No! You are not with me. You're not here. Having to deal with him. He can do his internship somewhere else. Not a store where we don't really have a manager. I can't even figure out how to stop the cheesecakes from coming. We've got the wrong pickles. And I don't have access to any ordering or delivery systems. Do you realize when I need more pickles, I have to pay in cash? I've got stupid sticky notes everywhere to keep track. This is no way to run a business. The last thing I need is a snot-nosed MBA coming in here and trying to tell me I'm doing it wrong. I *know* I'm doing it wrong. I don't have a choice!"

I realize everyone on staff is standing in the kitchen, staring at me through the open door of the manager's office.

Audra is quiet for a moment, then she says, "I can try talking to him, Nova. But he's determined to keep Jason there."

"Then you give Mr. Jace Pickle a message from me," I say, my voice low and threatening. "Until I speak to him directly, I will call the cops the first moment I see Jason Packwood enter this establishment. And if that's not good enough, he should remember the only thing standing between locking up his deli and shutting it down until he shows up to run it himself, is ME."

I hang up the phone.

Everyone still stares at me. Elda covers her mouth with her hand.

Of course they're anxious. I threatened their jobs.

Thinking about my own damn self.

I stand as straight as I can and walk between them, through the door and into the empty front room of the deli. I check that the doors are locked. That the sign is switched to closed. I run my hand along the sandwich line, waiting to be emptied and cleaned.

I stare at the cash register, wishing I could go back in time and redo that conversation. Not strike fear into the hearts of my crew.

But I did mean it. I can't keep going as if I'm in

charge. Jace Pickle needs to man up and talk to his acting manager.

And as for me, I need to work on my phone skills.

And my temper.

7

JACE

W ell, Audra isn't going to help anymore.

I hang up the phone and fall back onto the sofa in my condo.

Nova Strong threatened to shut down my deli. Could she do that?

As best as I can tell, I only have a couple of full-time employees and a handful of part-timers. Audra put in a couple of calls to the original manager, but in return only got identical auto-generated emails saying she's at a doctor's appointment.

Something is wrong. I know for a fact Susan has not stepped foot in her office for six months, and yet she's drawn her paycheck just the same. Audra forwarded all the pay receipts.

The lawyer has fired off a certified letter to Susan's address, letting her know she's being terminated. That should flush her out. It went to an Austin address, and if she's in Hawaii, no telling when she'll get it. But we have to do this by the book.

I don't bear any illusion that simply firing my manager is going to solve my problem. Even if we've been paying her not to be there, it doesn't change the fact that the budget should support her salary, no one else was getting it, and we have plenty of business to keep things going.

Something is wrong somewhere else. And that has to lie at the feet of Nova Strong.

I could fire her. Wipe the whole slate clean, shut down for a couple of weeks and start over with new staff.

But the truth is, I don't know how to do a damn thing. Watching Arush make the chicken salad, I realize I don't even know the ingredients. And the crew can set up the sandwich line in a heartbeat. I can't do that.

And truth be told, I don't buy that Nova is guilty. I don't want to believe it. She's smart and funny and competent as the leader.

I need to get back in there.

To do that, I have to let her talk to Jace Pickle.

But I can't. As soon as I say five words, she's going to know I'm him.

Damn it. I need someone to speak for me.

Whoever talks to her has to know the business inside and out. They have to be able to make decisions on the fly. And be persuasive.

I don't know anybody like that.

Or do I?

Shit, I do.

But it will totally suck to ask.

I have no choice.

I snatch up my cell phone and hit the speed dial.

Here goes nothing.

The line picks up. "Max Pickle."

My brother's voice is abrupt and baritone, closer to the sound of my dad than mine or Anthony's.

"Hey, it's Jace."

"What's up with the incognito call?"

I'd forgotten I hid my caller ID to avoid an accidental reveal.

"Woman problems. Listen, I need some help."

"Did I hear that correctly? Big brother Jace needs someone to help him?" He laughs.

"Can it."

"No. No, wait. Don't tell me. You hid your number. You have a woman problem. Did you finally tangle with some married chick and the husband's coming after you? Do you need your big buff brother to protect your skinny little ass?"

"I do not have a skinny little ass."

"I wouldn't know. I don't look at your ass."

"Max, can you shut the hell up? It's about my deli."

This admission gets just as big of a laugh. "You do need help. I saw your numbers. You couldn't sell hay to a cow."

"All right, all right. Have your fun at my expense."

"Thank you. I will."

"I don't see you in the lead. Anthony is kicking both our asses."

"As he should. He's the cuisine master of the family. Next to Grammy, anyway."

"Are you going to help me or not?"

"That depends. If you ask me to help you jump ahead of me in our little brother battle, you can shove it. You're sucking at it, and you deserve what you get. But if it's something else, we can talk."

I try to angle this to ensure Max will help me. "My manager's gone missing, and some hellfire chick has run my deli into the ground."

"Well, shit. How long has this been going on?"

"Too long." I have no intention of telling him I've been absent for over six months.

"What's your plan?"

"I convinced her to hire me under my real name so I could figure out where the money's going."

Max laughs so hard and so long I have to hold the phone away from my ear in frustration.

He finally manages to choke out, "So you're working in your own damn deli? As an employee? And let me guess. She fired you."

Why does everyone assume that?

"She caught me snooping and thinks I'm some corporate spy. I told her I was a friend of Jace. Now she insists on having Jace call her, but I can't call her, because I'm me."

"So you're trying to get back in there?"

"Exactly. I managed to get into the accounting folders to figure out what the hell was going on with my profits when she caught me."

"Jace, you're not using your head. If you want to look at the books, go there after hours. It's not as if the deli is open late. You don't have to work there to see what's going on."

"You're right about the computer, but I do have to be there. I've caught them opening the register to take out cash twice. And this acting manager hasn't had access to the books in months. So in addition to looking at the digital trail, I have to be there to see what the hell's going on inside the operation."

"You think they're stealing from you?"

"They have to be. That place is hopping. There's no reason we're practically in the red. I'll use the accounting files to make sure there's nothing weird with the profit and loss. But I have to be in the store to keep an eye on the employees themselves."

"Sounds like you're in a hell of a mess. What do you need me to do?"

"This acting manager, Nova Strong, wants to talk directly to Jace. I need someone to be me, someone who knows enough about the chain and the family to convince her this Jason guy is legit and, while possibly annoying, practically part of the family."

Max pauses a moment, then he says, "If I do this, do you swear you will not be so stupid as to blow your cover again by using your keys or passwords while there are other people around?"

"I will."

"You just do your job. Like an average Joe. And keep your eyes open."

"I will."

"I'll do this, not because I think you deserve it, or because you have been legitimately put upon by the deli you never even bother to visit. But your deli is part of our family business, and I don't like the idea of somebody stealing from it. So we all ought to pull together on something like that."

"Thank you."

"Forward me some information about this woman and what you want me to say."

"Thanks."

"And you tell me how this turns out. I don't want any of our stores falling apart."

"I hear you. Got it."

He hangs up, and I stare at the ceiling for a while.

Max is right on every count. I've let my deli go. I haven't paid attention. I haven't cared, and I should've. Because of that, everything's falling apart, and worst of all, I've disappointed Dad.

I'm going to fix this. The deli isn't so far gone that it can't be resurrected.

Max is good. He'll get me back in. This time I'll do whatever Nova Strong tells me to do. I'll snoop on my own time, keep my head down and eyes open.

And hopefully, I'll catch a thief.

And it won't be her.

I really hope it isn't her.

8

NOVA

The deli is different without Jason around. He'd only been there a day and a bit, but I feel his absence.

I don't know what it is. Maybe it was fun teaching someone who knew nothing. Maybe I like bossing around someone with money. I'm not so naïve as to think that didn't feel good.

But it seems like we have unfinished business.

And it's definitely *not* because of the hate spark. Although just thinking about it makes me rub my arm.

I have a full crew today, so I don't need any extra help. Arush takes over the chopping. Kate and Lamonte man the sandwich line. Elda keeps the tables moving. I get to feel like a manager, making sure things run smoothly, filling in where needed, and managing deliveries.

It's a good day, and our totals as we go into our last half hour before close are higher than average. I think about doing a free cheesecake promotion. I missed

Valentine's Day, but St. Patrick's Day is coming up. Maybe I can come up with something clever to put on the chalkboard easel out on the sidewalk. If I can get our averages up every day, maybe that will look good to somebody.

But who? Audra? The assistant? The invisible owner? The absent manager?

Who, exactly, am I doing this for?

The phone rings, but Kate is busy with a customer, so I pick it up myself.

"Austin Pickle, this is Nova."

"Oh, good. I caught you." It's Audra, Jace's assistant.

"I told you, I'm only going to speak to Jace."

"I have him on the line. I'll transfer you to him. I just wanted to start the call, so you knew it was him."

"Fine." I start rehearsing all the nasty, horrible things I want to say to him.

"I think you'll find he's nicer than you expect. He's just distracted."

"Put him on."

I hear a faint click, then a deep friendly voice fills my ear. "Nova Strong. I've been hearing a lot about you."

For some reason, my throat goes dry. I've never spoken directly to the owner. "I'm sure it's all terrible."

"Nothing of the sort. I understand my manager's gone AWOL, and the only reason the walls are still standing is because of you."

"I'm trying." I silently add, *no thanks to you.* Yes, I'm too chicken to say it out loud now that I'm actually speaking with Jace Pickle.

His voice is like melted butter. "I've been talking to accounting, and we are working with Susan to make her medical leave official. Since she's already been gone for six months, this opens up the management position, at least for the foreseeable future. I'd like to offer it to you, with your full title, and the full salary. Glancing at the balance sheets, it looks to be about a four hundred percent raise for you. Does that work?"

Four hundred percent raise.

He goes on. "It'll be salaried. Based on these timesheets in front of me, you've been working a lot of hours. In fact, it's more hours than Susan. So how about I throw in an extra five hundred dollars a month over what Susan was making, because you are more present than she was?"

Now my knees are weak. With that raise, I can go back to school.

Of course, I'm working full-time, which will make school hard. But I quickly run the math in my head. If I hold out for one year, I will save enough for tuition. Then I could go part-time again, at least to finish my undergrad. The master's degree would be more. But I can think about that later.

"Nova? You still there?"

"Yes."

"Do we have a deal?"

"Of course. And thank you. I didn't realize you were paying attention."

He chuckles. "Probably because I wasn't super available. I'll admit that straight out. I thought Susan was doing her job, and you all were holding down the fort beautifully. Turns out it was all you. I'm glad to get the opportunity to compensate you for that."

"Thank you."

"I'd like to talk to you a minute about Jason Packwood."

Oh, right. Him.

"He's more or less family, and we want to help set Jason on the right path. I probably should've sent him to one of my brothers' delis, but mine seemed to be doing so well. I thought it would be the perfect place for him to learn he's not the hotshot he thinks he is."

"I did manage to teach him how to dice onions."

"That's perfect." Jace lets out a deep-throated laugh. "You keep right on that. And since you're uncomfortable with him on the computer, I've withdrawn his access. That said, if you have some tips for him and want to show him some of the shipments and invoices, particularly now that you have access as manager, that would be helpful. Perhaps the two of you together could knock some ideas around. He's kinda wet behind the ears as far as manual labor, but he's really sharp."

That seems fair. "All right. I just worried he was a spy." Even as I say the words, I realize how ridiculous they sound.

"You were watching out for us, Nova. I appreciate that. I'll be sending some documents over by courier for you to sign for your new position. We will get you some back pay for at least the last, let's say ninety days, and hopefully, things will be looking up for Austin Pickle."

Wow. Back pay. "Thank you."

The line goes dead. I sit there, still holding the phone for a good thirty seconds.

Kate comes up behind me. "You look like you've seen a ghost."

I turn to her. "I think I just heard from one. That was Jace Pickle."

"What did he say?"

"He named me manager of the deli."

Kate squeals and runs to tell the others. I look around the store like I've never seen it before. I know I've been running the place for months, but now it's different. I'm actually in charge. And the owner talked to me. And he likes me. And he gave me a four hundred percent raise. And back pay. And a bonus.

None of this would've happened if Jason Packwood hadn't walked in and been a punk. We probably would've gone on and on the same way we were, forever.

It might be time to face some facts.

Jason Packwood is the best thing that's ever happened to me.

9

JACE

Well, my brother likes her.

I replay parts of the conversation with Max in my head as I wait at the back door of Austin Pickle for someone to answer the buzzer.

Max gave me the rundown of his conversation with Nova, including the rather generous compensation package he'd come up with on the fly. The price of his help, he claimed, was to make it up to this fiery lady, with the side benefit of making it harder for my deli to profit.

Not that Nova was being overpaid for a manager. In fact, she'd been pretty underpaid for the work she's been doing. She should have been at least pulling an assistant manager's salary.

Plus, he gave her back pay and a bonus. That was pure Max mischief. He's already had legal do the paperwork and courier it, along with authorization to have tech let her onto the network.

Yeah, it's going to be hard to pull ahead with all that. Good for Nova.

Bad for me.

I suppose at this point in the challenge, it isn't about winning. Well, it is. But I probably don't have a chance in hell.

It's about figuring out what's going wrong with my deli. And fixing it. It wouldn't surprise me to find out I'm so far behind the others I can't possibly catch up. The numbers the accountant sent us didn't lie.

I buzz again.

This time Lamonte opens the back door. "We don't want any," he says with a laugh.

When his remark causes me to take a step back, he chuckles again. "I'm kidding, man. You look as serious as a heart attack."

"How's Nova this morning?" I ask.

"You mean, does she seem in the killing mood? Like she might chop you to bits and mix your mangled body in the meat sauce?"

"Is it that bad?"

"Why don't you ask her yourself?"

We head inside. The entire crew is in the kitchen. They're clustered around several yellow buckets.

Elda dunks a plastic-gloved hand into one and pulls out a large green pickle. "Praise the Lord," she says. "We no longer have to stuff those teeny peckers."

Nova nods. She has her back to me. Today's ensemble is a sweet, form-fitted short-sleeved shirt and green camo pants. I try not to be too obvious admiring that sweet ass, but she looks around and catches me anyway.

"Jason," she says. At least she's dropped the bitter note. "Glad to have you back."

Okay. That's not too bad.

I wonder if Max left out anything they'd said to each other. Maybe he somehow turned me into a likable character.

I give her a quick nod. "Thank you for letting me return. I'm sorry I overstepped."

"I think we know where we stand, right?"

"We do."

I walk up to the line of buckets. "What's all this?"

Lamonte circles the table to the other side. He shoves a plastic glove on his hand and arranges a row of pickles, so they are lined up by size. "The minute Nova got access to the delivery system, she tracked down our original supplier of extra-large pickles for the stuffed dills. We've been struggling with a new company the last couple of weeks. Their pickles were too small."

"Pricks," Elda says.

Everyone erupts into giggles. It's apparently a favorite joke.

But this definitely interests me. "Somebody switched the pickles?"

Nova's fingers wrap around a particularly girthy specimen, and I have to steel my jaw to shove aside the untoward thoughts in my head.

Nova turns the pickle over. "Susan switched our provider." She lifts the pickle close to her face, taking a closer look. I have to take a deep breath and will my male anatomy to chill the hell out.

"Why would she do that?" I ask.

"They're bound to be cheaper," Lamonte says. "Maybe she was seeing something on the books that meant we weren't turning a profit on the stuffed ones."

"I doubt that woman cared one whit," Elda says with a snort.

"I'll try to take a look tonight," Nova says. "There's a lot to untangle from the books."

"How did you get new pickles so fast?" I ask.

"I called first thing this morning. Austin is a regional distributor for these, so I was able to get someone out right away. They were very happy to get our business back."

She sets down the pickle and glances at me. "Don't stand around being pointless. Get an apron on. Back to dicing."

"My nemesis," I say, and the crew laughs again. My gut tightens. I've never felt camaraderie with a group like this before. It's interesting and new.

It feels good.

Except Nova. She watches me warily, as if she doesn't quite trust I'm there to work.

I'll have to prove her wrong. I need to earn all of these people's trust.

I can't count on the AWOL manager being the crux of the problem with my deli. And it's possible Max gave a giant raise to the very person who's causing my deli to go under.

But all this will remain to be seen.

The group disperses as I slide on an apron. Lamonte puts away the pickles. "You can find the bin of onions for today's chopping in the front of Mr. Chill."

"Mr. Chill?"

"The big fridge."

"What do you guys call the freezer? Mr. Freeze?"

"No, we call that JP."

"What's it stand for?"

Lamonte shakes his head. "Jace Pickle. Look, I know you're friends with the boss man and all, but you've got to know, up until yesterday, when he promoted Nova, he wasn't too popular around here."

I accept that. And hopefully, as soon as all this is done, I'll find a way to fix it. Nova won't be too happy when she figures out that the Jason she's had in her deli has been Jace Pickle all along, but there will be no getting around telling her in the end.

I realize Lamonte is still standing there, looking at me like I've turned to stone.

I shake my thoughts loose. "Wait. What does the freezer have to do with Jace Pickle?"

He takes his time screwing the lid back onto one of the yellow buckets. "You don't get it? We named the freezer JP after the son of a bitch who left us out in the cold."

Point taken.

10

NOVA

Jason Packwood appears to be as good as his word.

For the next week, he's a model employee. He chops onions and jalapeños without complaint. He refills the sandwich line during the rush. He washes dishes.

Arush teaches him how to make the famed chicken salad. Now that Jason's got the onion dicing down, my best cook seems to have taken him under his wing. They're at it again today, with Jason mixing the ingredients.

All is well.

I walk through the kitchen and into Susan's office.

Or, I guess, *my* office.

I spin around in the chair. I haven't changed anything since I was named acting manager. I haven't had time. In fact, the paper Jason tacked up is still there, too.

Going through the books looking for abnormalities

and catching up on six months of memos from the franchise is taking up all my free time.

Anthony Pickle, the brother who owns the franchise in Colorado, has a test kitchen where they create new breads for the sandwiches, as well as the pickle of the month, and any specialty items to serve seasonally.

We've missed almost all those opportunities from corporate since the emails were going into the black hole of Susan's manager account.

But now I can see them all.

We've been doing the pickle of the month, because the vats arrive from Colorado, and we put them out with signage that this is a temporary pickle flavor.

But I had no idea about the different breads.

We normally serve three kinds. A fortified white, whole wheat, and rye.

But once I see the other recipes with light-hearted, clever names, I vaguely remember from my early days that we would occasionally have a specialty bread and a sale associated with it.

We missed the fall bread with cranberry for the holidays, called "Rudolph's Nose." And the winter bread with walnuts and pecans called "Go Nuts."

But the new spring bread looks to be a lot of fun. Anthony has outdone himself.

Normally the breads are baked early each day. But this new one needs to be tested in our kitchen before introducing it to the line.

And making bread is tedious, the perfect job for someone who needs to be taught patience.

I glance through the open door of my office into the

kitchen. Arush and Jason are finishing up the chicken salad. Arush will move onto the sandwich line with Kate. Eli is here today to run the refills from the fridge to the line. And Elda, of course, always keeps the tables clear and makes sure the beverage counter is clean and functional.

Arush says something to Jason I can't hear, and they laugh. Both are good-looking men, Arush's dark hair and heavy eyebrows enigmatic and fun. With Jason's model-perfect face and haircut, the two of them look like they're shooting the pilot for the next streaming television sensation.

Jason's demeanor is much easier around Arush than me. He looks almost casual, like he could be a normal human and not some rich boy playing a role for kicks.

Kate pops through the swinging door, and I watch carefully to see how the men respond to her. Arush suddenly goes quiet and serious, as if her arrival is something sacred. He drops a spoon on the floor with a clatter of metal. His face turns bright red as he bends down to retrieve it, then he bumps his head on the table on his way back up.

Jason notices it like I do, looking between Arush and Kate.

"Hey, Arush! Hey, Jason!" Kate's blond ponytail swings as she waves. "Where's Nova?"

"In the office," Jason says. He saves the giant vat of chicken salad from certain doom when Arush nearly drops it. "Whoa, there, Arush. You're on a roll."

Kate shakes her head as she moves my way. I wonder why I've never noticed Arush's apparent crush on Kate. Probably because I've had my focus on one crisis after another. But the crew is good right now. I can rely on them.

And I'm finally getting paid for what I do.

Things are good.

Kate approaches the door. "Knock, knock!"

"Hey."

"So, the pickle of the month came in, but we don't have a spot for it. Remember the cooling thingamajig broke on the last row?"

"Right. Hey, I can get it fixed now." I spin around in the chair and pull up the *Service Provider* folder on the computer. "If we don't already have a repair person, I'll find one. Just stow the vat in Mr. Chill and we'll start the pickle of the month when it's fixed."

I make a note on a sticky to call for repairs and realize Kate is still standing in the doorway.

"Is there something else? We have fifteen minutes until we open."

Kate examines her pink fingernails. "I was going to ask you about Jason."

Great. Does she want to date him? I've seen the clean-up girls giggling over him.

"You don't need my blessing to ask him out," I say.

"What? No! I mean, no!" She glances behind her and shakes her head. "No, no. Not my type."

"Really?"

"I mean, he's good-looking and all. But he seems a little too much. I don't think I could date someone who wears thousand-dollar jeans."

"What?" I look around her to spy on Jason's pants.

"Fendi. Look them up. I had no idea, but Lamonte seems to know all about them. He's lusted after a pair since middle school, apparently."

"Why would anyone spend that much money on jeans?"

"I guess when you've got it, you spend it."

"That's a whole month's rent!"

Kate turns to survey Jason as he washes the mixing bowls in the sink. His back is to us. "I guess there's no price on making a butt look that good."

She has a point.

Kate takes a couple of steps inside. "I was talking to Elda yesterday, and she agrees. He's been looking at you."

"He can look all he wants, but he's not my type either." I remember for a moment that spark when we touched. Nope. No way. Hate spark.

Although it's probably toned down to a glow of annoyance.

"I figured. Poor little rich boy. I bet the customers will eat him up if you ever put him on the sandwich line." Kate tilts her head. "Are you?"

I tear my eyes away from Jason's butt and ask, "Am I what?"

"Uh huh. I thought so."

Now she has my attention. "You thought what?"

"Never mind." Her happy grin makes her look like a fresh-faced girl in a magazine ad. "Want me to unlock the front door?"

I glance at the clock on the computer. It's time. "Sure. I'll be out there before it gets hectic."

"You always are!" She flips her ponytail and heads out.

Jason finishes washing the bowl and sets it on a drying rack. He opens the industrial dishwasher and starts pulling plates for the lunch run.

He's got the hang of the routine.

And I have to admit, he's working hard.

"Hey, Jason," I call out, then realize my mouth got ahead of my brain.

He turns around. "What's up?"

I guess I'm committed. "Come here!"

He stops in the doorway of the office and leans against the frame. "What can I do for you, boss?"

I stifle a completely inappropriate reply. "You know how to make bread?"

"Nope."

"Well, today you're going to learn."

"During the lunch rush?"

"I'll get you started, and I assume you'll be able to watch dough rise while we serve?"

"Sure."

"Pull all the usual ingredients for the white bread. It's the base for the new one. We'll add the special ingredients before we let it rise."

"Will do. I assume we're not using this bread today?"

I glance at the memo. "This says the start date is Monday. We're closed on Sundays, which means we have today and tomorrow to get this bread perfected and ready to go on the line. We'll do the first run today.

I'll start the early run tomorrow to fix anything that goes wrong today."

"Aye, aye, captain. Should I come early too?"

"We'll decide based on how it goes today."

Jason gives me a mock salute as he heads over to Bertha, the mega-pantry that holds the dry stock.

And I have to admit Kate is right.

His butt does look good in thousand-dollar jeans.

11

JACE

Nova watches me as I bend over a giant stainless-steel bowl, up to my elbows in a floury paste. So far, my first lesson in bread making has been a disaster. Both of my early attempts ended up in the garbage.

"Does this dough look right?" I ask.

I'm trying not to stare at her, although I could use the distraction from my failures. Her camo pants are pink today, and her round little ass juts out perfectly as she leans over the table to supervise my work. She has a dusting of flour on her nose.

"You haven't screwed this one up—yet," she says, her voice laced with annoyance. She's so short, she has to stand on a stool to see over the edge of the bowl. "But it's pretty wet."

Now that gets my imagination going.

It doesn't help that she sticks her hands inside the wad of dough next to mine. It's like the pottery scene from *Ghost*. Warm, soft, malleable...

Nova's hard voice cuts my fantasy short. "It's not ready. Keep kneading."

Dang. She's a hard ass.

Our hands touch inside the dough and she jerks hers out so fast her plastic glove remains behind. "You're on your own." She reaches inside the bowl and tugs out the errant glove, refusing to meet my gaze.

What just happened there?

"I don't think I can do it alone."

She's angry at me, I guess due to my incompetence, and waves the glove in my face. "You think I knew how to make bread when I got here? Learn, Peckerwood."

"It's Packwood."

"You're lucky I don't call you limp biscuit!" She flounces out.

Damn, but I will never figure her out.

I keep squishing the dough. The first batch didn't rise. Apparently putting the sugar on top of the yeast is a big no-no. The second batch got lumpy because the water I added was warm. Nobody told me the temperature mattered.

So far, this one is too wet and sticky. If I botch a third one, it'll prove I'm incompetent to Nova. I'm determined to get this one right.

I knead the dough carefully. Not too much force. Not too little. I know it shouldn't stick to my hands or the sides of the bowl.

It's oddly relaxing, making bread. I can picture Grammy Alma doing it. Actually, maybe I can call Grammy about this.

No one's currently in the kitchen, although Eli

makes runs back and forth from Mr. Chill to the sandwich line. I bet I can get a quick call off.

It's one-thirty in New York. The lunch rush should be settling down there. Grammy will take my call regardless, though.

I tug out my phone and hit the speed dial.

She answers on the second ring. "Baby J!" she calls. "What's wrong?"

"Nothing," I say. "Is it crazy there?"

"Nothing Sunny and the crew can't handle. What's going on?"

"I'm at Austin Pickle, and I'm trying to make bread."

Grammy laughs in a deep, low chuckle. "You? Making bread?"

"I know. I know. I'm trying to learn. But it keeps failing."

"What's it doing?"

"The first one didn't rise."

"You put sugar on top of the yeast?"

"Yeah." Of course she'd know.

"The second?"

"Warm water."

"Rookie mistake. What's wrong with this one?"

"It's too sticky. I followed the instructions."

"What's the humidity there?"

"I don't know."

"Well, check!"

I shift to a weather app. "Oh. One hundred percent." I can't see outside from here. "I guess it's raining."

"There you go. Slowly add a tablespoon of flour at a time to compensate for the extra moisture in the air."

"How will I know when it's enough?"

"It won't stick, and it will start to make a little skin."

"Okay."

"Call me back if you run into more trouble."

"Thanks, Grammy."

"I'm proud of you. Good luck." She hangs up.

Proud. I wonder when the last time a member of my family has said that to me.

I add a bit of flour to the dough and push it into the ball, then roll it forward like Nova showed me.

I used to be the favored son. The eldest. The pride and joy. Then I left for college, got into the scene there, and shifted gears. Quit caring so much. By then, Dad was funneling profits from his Manhattan Pickle into our accounts, so working didn't matter. But when he started scouting for a location for Austin Pickle, I realized my future wasn't my own.

I guess I rebelled.

I'm still rebelling at thirty.

I realize I've automatically added another spoonful of flour and the dough has stopped sticking.

Nova wanders back into the kitchen. "Hey, that dough looks good!"

"Yeah, I think it's ready." I try not to let my voice reveal how chuffed I feel.

"Looks like it's time to knead in the final ingredient."

"Sure. What's that?"

"Pickles."

Wait, what?

"Why would you add pickles to perfectly good bread?"

"It's a specialty bread."

Damn. I've owned this deli for eight years and grew up sitting on the stool at my father's store. But I've never eaten any bread with pickles in it.

"Is it new?"

"All the branches are doing it."

This is probably my brother Anthony's doing. He's always the innovator.

Nova lifts the bag of flour, which holds down a printout of a recipe. "You'll need to chop two kosher dills."

"Dill pickles in bread?"

"That's what it says."

"And people eat it?"

"I think it's going to be hugely popular. But it might be the name."

"It has a name?"

Nova spins around to stare at me. "You never eat at any of the Pickles? Specialty breads are part of the chain's appeal."

I shrug. It's true I avoid our own delis. I got sick of it growing up. "There's lots of restaurants around town."

She shakes her head. "I think people are going to order this one just to say the name out loud."

Now she has me curious. "So, what's it called?"

"It's dill pickles and bread." She laughs. "What do you think?"

"I think I have no idea."

She leans in. "It's called the Dill Dough."

She's so close I can smell all the unique scents of her. Fresh bread. Dijon. A hint of dill. And underneath, something gently floral, her shampoo, maybe, or a body lotion.

I force my throat to swallow.

She taps the printout with her finger. "Funny, huh? The other Pickle brother is hilarious."

"Anthony? Definitely."

She stops at that. "How well do you know the Pickles?"

I have to take care with this answer, but her closeness has got me off balance. "I've been around the family all my life."

"Huh. Jace seemed all right when I finally talked to him."

She means Max. This is a tangled mess. I don't want to make her too curious about us. All she has to do is Google her boss and she'll clearly see it's me. I never expected to be here more than a day or two, much less a week and a half.

But I'm no closer to figuring out what's wrong with my deli.

"The brothers are cool," I say carefully. "I'll go get the dills from Mr. Chill."

When I return from the fridge, Nova has moved on.

I chop up the pickles to add to the bread, feeling uncertain about why I'm here.

I can come in and review the books any time I want. But I haven't.

And since Nova's been manager, there hasn't been anything weird about the register, as far as I can tell.

Is it because she thinks I'm a spy?

Or because there was never anything wrong?

With the other manager out of the picture, we should be pulling a good profit, even with her raise.

As I chop the pickle for the Dill Dough, I realize I need to ask myself the question: Why am I still here?

But the answer comes easily.

I'm not ready to leave Nova Strong.

12

NOVA

I just did something really stupid.

I guess it's not the *stupidest* thing. I didn't throw myself at a married man, for example. Or wash my whites with reds and turn everything pink.

But I did tell Jason Packwood to come early so we could do the next test run on the pickle bread before the rest of the crew arrived.

And here's the real problem.

I didn't even need to.

The third batch he did came out great. We sliced it up and passed it around. Everyone thought it was a great bread, something that could permanently go on the menu.

Jason did it well.

When I walk up to the back entrance of the deli at seven in the morning, Jason is already there. A fine spring mist is falling, typical for Austin in mid-March.

He's ditched the high-end jeans. And his stiff new T-shirts have gone soft from repeated washings.

He's starting to look more Austin. More regular guy, and not fancy pants.

Not that it matters. I'm still not interested. I can't be. I'm his boss.

Not that I have any delusions about the importance of a deli manager. And technically, he's an unpaid intern of sorts and can leave whenever he wants.

But I do tell him what to do, and if he's trying to impress the Pickle family, for whatever reason, I do wield some power over him.

So he's off-limits.

As I approach to unlock the door, he gives me a deep formal bow, hand wave and all, as he bends down. "My lord and master," he says. "I am ready to absorb more knowledge from your wise presence."

There he goes again. The over-the-top charm.

Although, for all the pomp and flourish, he seems oddly authentic. Like he means what he says, and he can't help it he's irresistible while doing it. I don't sense any purposeful attempt to manipulate me.

I shove the key in the lock. "All right, all right. Enough already."

"I only speak the truth."

I push open the door, the familiar scent of bread and pickle juice as familiar as home. I tuck my keys into my hoodie pocket.

I step aside to let him in. "This morning I'm here to see what *you* know. You are the one who made the perfect Dill Dough yesterday."

Jason's face lights up with a grin that's become unsettlingly familiar. I admit, I said the name of the bread more than necessary yesterday just to see his smile.

"We're making naughty, naughty things in the kitchen," he says with a wink.

I feel a bright warmth in my chest, like someone has lit a match.

I can't fool myself this time. It's not a hate spark.

I break out my deli manager tone. "You fetch the ingredients, and I'll get the proofing oven prepped."

"Your wish is my command."

He heads off to Bertha, and I attempt to shake off the happy glow as I adjust the settings on the special cabinet that holds the dough at the right temperature and humidity to rise properly.

We'll make another round of Dill Dough, and then I'll start the regular bread for the day.

I wonder if Jason could be my baking partner on the days Lamonte has off.

No, no.

There's no point in seeking more time with Jason Packwood. I'm not in his league. He's rich, on his way up, and temporary.

And I'm his boss. How many times do I need to remind myself of that?

Jason arrives with the dry goods. I head to Mr. Chill. When I return to the kitchen, Jason has already started measuring out the ingredients.

He's muttering to himself.

I catch a few words. "Sugar. Yeast. Check the humidity."

I drop the milk and butter on the table. "Everything okay?"

He nods. "Trying not to screw this up."

"What's that about humidity?"

Grammy told me to make sure I check it, so the dough won't be sticky," he says, then his eyes go wide. "I mean, my grandmother."

"I think it's cute you still call her Grammy." I open a block of butter to cut into pieces so it will soften faster. "Is she great at baking bread?"

He hesitates, then says, "Definitely. Some of my favorite memories from childhood are her baking." He quickly adds, "For fun. Just for family."

I frown at his awkward addition. Is he trying to hide the fact that his grandmother had a normal job? Maybe their family money didn't come until the next generation. But I don't pry. It isn't any of my business, even though I would love to know more about him.

"Is she the reason you want to go into the restaurant business?"

"Something like that."

I open another block of butter. "My mom can't cook spaghetti," I say. "I had to learn at a pretty early age, or my baby sister and I would've starved."

"You have a little sister?"

"She's only ten."

"Do they live here in town?"

I should have known he would ask this. I've kept my personal life away from the deli as much as possible. I don't like people feeling sorry for me.

I keep my answer simple. "They do. Leah's in fourth grade."

"Well, if she's anything like you, I bet she's a pistol."

"No, she's super sweet. She'd be the sort of girl to bring cards and cookies to someone who sliced their finger on a paper cutter, even if it was their own damn fault."

He grins at me. "Good to know I can count on one of the Strong girls."

"Oh, she's not a Strong."

Shut up, Nova. I don't need to bring that up.

But Jason skips right through it. "No brothers?"

"No, just Leah."

I focus on cutting the butter into neat, evenly sized bits. I desperately want to turn the conversation away from me. "Do you have any brothers or sisters?"

He hesitates, and I wonder if the question is too personal. "I have brothers," he finally says. "We live all over the place."

"Where did you grow up?"

"New York." He focuses on sifting the flour into the bowl, his lips pursed in concentration. I take that as a cue to stop talking.

We work in companionable silence. It's different from my early mornings with Lamonte, when we're always full of jokes and laughter and silliness.

Jason and I both reach for the bag of flour at the same time, and our hands brush.

Another spark.

Our eyes meet, and my head swirls. There's practically a chick-flick soundtrack in the background.

Jason withdraws his hand. "Ladies first."

"Don't call me a lady," I snap.

"Sorry," he says, although he doesn't sound the least bit sorry. "Give me the damn flour, wench."

I've just picked up the plastic tub when he also grabs for it. The container tilts, and flour spills over the edge, dropping onto the counter and billowing up.

We both let go, causing it to tumble, and a giant cloud of flour puffs into the air.

Soon we're coughing, coated in flour, and our pale faces turn to each other through the haze.

Jason cracks up first. "You look like a ghost."

"You look like a White Walker from Game of Thrones."

His laughter is infectious, and when the giggles start, I can't stop them.

Jason claps his hands together, sending another poof of flour into the air. This strikes us both as even more hysterical, and soon we're both doubled over, every shake of our bodies causing another flurry of flour.

I suck in air, realize its full of dust, and begin coughing. Jason smacks me on the back, then he starts coughing. Then I'm coughing harder. Then we're both laughing and coughing and coughing and laughing, until we finally stumble out the back door of the deli, gasping for fresh air.

The alley is quiet, although a few other businesses are also beginning their morning routine. A man steps out from the pizza place next door to see who is making the racket. We wave him off, trying desperately to sober up.

Finally, Jason asks, "Should we get back in there and clean up our mess?"

"Yeah. We're going to be off schedule soon."

"How about I continue with the pickle bread, and you start on the regular loaves?"

"That's a plan," I say. "Saturdays are pretty slow, at least. I don't have to make as many loaves as a weekday."

Jason looks thoughtful. "Should the deli close on Saturdays? Does it make financial sense to stay open if there's not much business?"

I move the compost bin to the edge of the table and scrape the spilled flour into it. "It's not my call to make. We do cut the crew. I feel like if we're making a profit at all, we should be open, because from what I've seen, once the business starts cutting its hours, the odds that the location will completely close inside of a year go up dramatically."

"Really?" Jason snatches up a broom to tackle the floor. "But what if they're doing it to get more streamlined? To improve the bottom line?"

I shrug. "It has to do with customer confidence. They no longer know for sure if the business will be open when they want to visit it. They're less likely to venture out. Anyway, didn't your professors go over that in business school? Where did you get your business degree?"

Jason's jaw tightens, and I wonder what that's all about. Does he not want to admit where he went to school?

"Up north," he says, but doesn't elaborate.

Maybe it was some crapola college.

He sweeps the flour into a pan. "How far along are you in your classes at UT?"

"About halfway."

"Why did you stop?"

The dreaded question has arrived. I wipe down the counter and decide to straight-up tell the truth. "I ran out of money."

Jason pauses, dustpan in hand. "You didn't want to take out student loans?"

I don't know how to explain this without seeming like a hot mess. I toss the rag into the sink and draw a mixing bowl close. "I burned through all of those. I can't take out anymore. I have to save money for tuition."

Jason dumps the flour into the compost. "But you work full-time. How will you go to class?"

"With the raise I got, I'll be able to save money. Hopefully, in a year or so, we can train another manager and I can go back to school."

I don't want to talk about this anymore. I concentrate on separating the butter into the right portions.

But Jason isn't letting it go. "I thought you could get whatever student loans you needed. Are you worried you won't be able to earn enough to pay them off?

"I had to use them for something else, okay? So back off."

I don't look at him. I didn't mean to snap like that, but the rich boy needs to shut up. He's probably never had to take out a loan. Or have a school question the use of funds when you're late on tuition.

We work in silence for a while, and the camaraderie evaporates. My upset hangs between us like a cloud.

I steal a tiny glance at Jason. He seems focused on the task of sifting flour.

"So exactly how do you compensate for the humidity?" I ask. It's the best I can do as an olive branch.

I already know how to do it. But it's conversation.

"If it's wet after you've mixed it, add a tablespoon of flour at a time. "Yesterday I had to add two tablespoons to the recipe to get the right consistency."

His voice has a husky quality, and I wonder if he's disgusted with me for overreacting.

"You might want to make a note on the sheet. That way the Monday crew knows what to do."

"I'm happy to come make it Monday morning," he says. "You want it to be perfect on the first day."

"It's nice of you to offer."

We're talking normally at last. I measure out baking powder into my bowl.

"I'm trying to absorb all I can," he says. "Honestly, my family thinks I'll never settle down enough to do any meaningful work."

Interesting. Sounds like he's aware of what Jace Pickle told me about him. Audra, too.

I lean on the counter and watch his hand knead the dough. "I don't know which is harder," I say. "Having your family expect great things from you and fail…" I pause for a second, brushing a smear of flour off my sleeve. "Or having the world expect nothing from you and trying to make something of yourself anyway."

Jason turns to me. "Why would anyone expect

anything less than amazing from you? You're smart and fiery and strong. You're a great leader. The crew here loves you. You're probably the best thing that's ever happened to this deli."

I didn't expect praise from him. "I don't exactly come from much. My mom works at a dollar store. I've never in my whole life owned more than two pairs of shoes." I glance down at my Army boots. "I buy them sturdy, so they last."

Jason sets down his sifter. "But you got into business school. At UT. That's hard to do. You should be proud of yourself."

"And I had to quit because I couldn't manage the loans. How can I manage a business if I can't even manage my life?"

I don't look at him, snatching up the sifter to add flour to my own bowl.

"Did you apply for scholarships? Isn't there aid for you?"

Rich kid has no idea. I set down the sifter and look him straight in the eye. "I don't think you understand the level of privilege you live in. Poor people don't know how to fill out Pell Grant forms. And at the time I was doing it, I didn't even have a permanent address. We moved from sofa to sofa, sometimes getting a ratty hotel room if no one would take us. We almost never had our own place for more than a month before Mom couldn't pay the rent. We kept all our things in trash bags, in case we had to take off before we got evicted."

Jason tries to hold my eyes, but they keep dipping to the table.

"It's hard to have a high school counselor help you through this process when you change schools every few weeks. I got lucky at one, and the counselor got me a bus pass so I could stay at the same school my senior year. They helped me write some essays that got me in. But it was too late for most of the deadlines for the big grants. So I took out student loans."

"And what happened to that money?"

I can't meet his gaze so I run my thumb along the handle of the sifter instead. "The first round went to tuition. But I needed to live somewhere. I couldn't abandon my mom and sister. So I used the rest to get us an apartment. A permanent place to live. Mom found the checkbook, and she decided she wanted to buy things she'd never had. We'd never had a television. She'd never had a cell phone. And she could buy clothes for my sister. She went through it."

"But that's theft. You didn't report her?"

"She's my mother, Jason." My throat tries to close. "Who's to say I deserve the money for myself? It made sense to let her use some of it. Most of it."

"Nova, I'm sorry—"

"No. Do not pity me. I made choices. And now I'm here. So don't feel sorry for me. I have a decent job, and the pay is finally okay. I can help my family, and I'm doing fine."

I fill the sifter and shake it fiercely. "If it's okay with you, I need to focus on making this bread. I'm half an hour behind, and I need fresh loaves ready for the sandwich line by eleven o'clock."

To his credit, Jason turns to his bowl and resumes his work.

I'm angry with myself. I don't tell my life story to anyone. They don't need to know.

I'm tough. And I've got this.

The only Nova anybody needs to know is the Strong one.

13

JACE

On Sunday morning, I decide I can't put it off any longer. I need to head up to my deli and start going through the books to figure out what's wrong.

As I drive my BMW through the quiet streets of downtown, Nova Strong and her tough situation are heavy on my mind.

It's a lot. On one hand, I'm extremely sympathetic. She was right to call me out on my privilege. I never even saw a tuition bill when I was in school. I've never written a rent check. Audra pays my bills for me, and I've never questioned my ability to cover them. Well, other than a few seconds when my life flashed before my eyes as my dad told us about the profit challenge.

I'm not even sure where I am with that right now. It's all so tangled. Nova. The deli. The crew.

But Nova was very clear in her confession that she mismanages money. She used student loans on things other than school. There's no telling what justification she might have created in her mind for taking money from the deli. She was grossly underpaid, that's for sure. She's susceptible to sob stories, like her mother. And Lamonte's gas money.

I need to assess the damage that's been done.

And make sure it's not still happening.

I find street parking around the corner from the front door. The late morning is chilly, and I have to peer through the low-hanging fog. I stand in front of the plate glass windows for a moment, looking up at the green-and-white-striped awning, the bold black letters that read *Austin Pickle.*

This is my store. My legacy. I never thought much about it in all the years since it opened, but now I do.

It doesn't just feed people, it employs people. It keeps Lamonte in Converse and Netflix. Kate hopes to save enough to travel around Europe this summer. Arush is building a savings account to start his own little hole-in-the-wall restaurant. He spins his dreams about it while mixing my grandmother's chicken salad.

I hope I can clear Nova of wrongdoing. I want to find big chunks of stolen money hidden in the delivery and orders that I can trace back to the old manager.

I really, really do.

I unlock the front door to breathe in the crisp, pine-scented clean of the restaurant. I turn to make sure it's locked tight before wandering through the empty tables, chairs stacked on top. The brushed metal counter of the sandwich line shines from the muted light coming through the window.

I pause by the swinging door and look back at the expansive room. It's in good shape, everything kept up, clean, and bright. It's a place to be proud of.

I turn to push through the door, when I realize a light is on in the kitchen.

My muscles tense as I realize somebody's here.

I peer through the window. The kitchen itself is empty, the cabinets clear, all the dishes put away.

But Nova's office door is open.

Did she close and lock it before we left? I search for the memory, but I'm not sure.

Could she be here?

Foreboding washes over me. Who else would be here? And what would they be doing? Covering tracks? Stealing more?

I push on the door, wincing at the squeak. It seems to shriek in the quiet.

I peer through the window. Still no sign of anyone.

I push a little more and squeeze through.

I'm out in the open now. Not all the kitchen lights are on. The washing station is dim, and so is the cutting table. The pantry is closed up. It's the switch by the back door that's been flipped.

And Nova's office. Light spills from the cocked door.

Whoever's here can answer to me. But I would like to know, preferably before they see me.

I think I'm about to catch a thief.

I'm glad for my sneakers as I creep across the floor toward Nova's office. Now that I'm close, I can hear papers shuffling, and the occasional click of the keyboard.

I can't see the desk from this angle, so I slowly advance through the kitchen until I'm almost at the door.

Then I hear a long sigh of frustration.

I'd know that sound anywhere.

It's Nova.

I halt, listening.

"Why would she do that?" Nova's voice is laced with annoyance. "Who do I call to fix this?"

She's upset. I can only assume she's referring to Susan, the former manager. And I do recall Nova saying she had been picking through Susan's decisions to figure out why deliveries had been changed, and why we were overstocked on some things and short on others.

I don't step forward enough to see her, because she might turn and spot me, but I do listen a moment more.

Nova thinks out loud. "All right, here's the dessert order. I can get that stopped. She increased it before she left. But I don't remember selling that many back then. I need to find the files from the register. Did we use the software then? When did we switch over? God, this is a mess."

She's figuring it out.

I lean against the wall. I shouldn't have doubted her. She wants my deli to do well. She's not going to do anything to put it in peril. She's solving the mystery, just like I am.

I need to back away. Get home. Think. Should I tell her who I am so we can work together on this?

Am I sure enough to do that?

I take a slow, easy step toward the swinging door, but

my sneaker slips on a well-waxed bit of tile. The squeak breaks the silence like a dog toy in the night.

A rolling sound probably means Nova heard and has pushed away from her desk.

I quickly dash around the corner that frames her office so she can't spot me easily.

"Is someone out there?" she calls.

Shit. Shit. Shit. I race through scenarios of what I can say. The Pickles gave me a key. I want to practice the bread one more time before Monday.

Maybe I can confess I'm snooping again. Say I'm sorry. That I'll leave.

But I discard those ideas. If I'm caught again, I have to fess up. Tell her I'm Jace.

She'll hate me then.

Shit.

Nova calls out again. "Anyone there?"

A sound like springs squeaking comes from her direction, and I'm guessing she's stood up.

Thank goodness for her heavy boots. I can hear two distinct steps, then silence.

I breathe long and slow, and as silently as possible. If I can get out of here, I can stay Jason. Stay working at Austin Pickle. But if she catches me, we're through. The way she blew up the last time she caught Jason snooping, and with her newfound power as manager and connection with Max, who she thinks is me, she'll feel empowered to throw Jason out.

I can almost hear the conversation: *"I gave it a shot. He was good at making the bread. I think he's gotten a decent feel for what it's like to be among the crew. You guys need to take it from here."*

And Max won't argue. He'll tell her to kick me out, and then call and insist I end the ruse.

Damn it.

It's about to be over. All of it. The ability to work for her. Making bread. Seeing her with flour on her nose.

I realize none of those thoughts involve the accounting problem with my deli.

It's her.

Damn it.

I want to be with her.

Nova does not appear in the kitchen. I don't know how long she stays looking out her door, but eventually the footsteps recede inside the office, and the spring in her chair squeaks again.

When the wheels roll and paper rustles, I know I'm safe.

Nothing has to change.

I have to get out of here. At the first tap of her keyboard, I move quickly toward the swinging door. I slide through it silently and make sure it doesn't move when I'm past. Then I race to the front door, open the lock, push through, turn to lock it again, and sprint away from the glass windows.

Only when I've turned the corner and am out of sight of the front door, do I pause to take a breath.

And decide it's time to admit a few things.

My head knows what my heart has been feeling all along. Nova is not my deli's problem.

We're in this together.

And I start to think maybe it doesn't matter what happened in the past.

I want to work with her to make my deli improve.

I want to work with *her*.

14

NOVA

If we had an employee of the month, it just might be Jason Packwood.

You can knock me over with a feather on that, because I never would have dreamed Mr. Rich Boy Fancy Pants would start showing up at the crack of dawn to make sure the bread at the deli is perfect.

He's also become best friends with Arush. The two of them have gotten thick as thieves over the sweetness of onion varieties and the potency of pickle juice.

It's insane.

But there's more.

A lot more.

Sometimes in the middle of the mad lunch rush, when I'm pitching in at the register, or slapping pastrami on a slice of rye, I'll catch him watching me while he slides a new vat of pickle relish on the sandwich line.

It's little things. Like him noticing when I'm too tired to be wielding a knife to catch us up on the tomato slices, so he takes over even though he ought to be done.

And last week when a customer got in my face, angry we were out of Dill Dough and he had to accept plain bread on his sandwich, Jason easily slid into the situation and placated the man when I was about to smack him with salami.

Sometimes I wonder if he's *really* always there when I need a helping hand, or if I'm *looking* for him to be there.

It's a Friday near the end of March and, Connie, one of the two cleanup girls, calls in sick with the flu.

My other girl, Charlotte, shows up looking like death.

"I think you have it, too," I tell her. "You need to go home."

"You can't have us both out," Charlotte insists before succumbing to what feels like a six-hour coughing fit.

I walk her to the door. "I can't have you keeling over. Let me pack up the leftover soup of the day to send with you. Call me when you're better."

"I can't afford to lose the hours." She gazes up at me, eyes wet, nose red.

I completely understand what that's like.

"I'll find an extra hour of work for you to do each day when you're better. We'll make them up so your paycheck's the same. Okay?"

She nods and shuffles to a chair while I dump the pot of chicken noodle in a plastic container for her to take home.

When I safely have her out the door, I turn around to face the extra work.

Regular staff handles all the pots and dishes after

clearing the deli line. But the cleanup girls do the bathrooms and mop the floors.

Looks like I'm doing that today.

I've just filled the mop bucket with sudsy water when Jason emerges from Bertha.

"What are you doing here?" I ask.

"I was rearranging some of the ingredients. A delivery came in, and we needed to rotate the stock."

I nod. "Thanks for being a self-starter on that. Sometimes I feel overwhelmed by all the details."

"You got a spill you need to take care of?" He gestures at the mop.

"Both of the cleaning crew are down with the flu. So, I'm it."

I push the rolling bucket toward the swinging door.

"What all is there to do?" he asks. "I can help."

Yeah right. It's one thing for Fancy Pants to chop onions and bake bread. It's a whole different thing to scrub a toilet. "That's not necessary. You're not even paid help. I did call Audra about that, but she said you weren't interested in money."

"That's true. And I'm not too good to clean up."

"You're going to disinfect a toilet bowl?"

He doesn't hesitate. "My hands work as well as anybody's."

I'm not going to turn him down. "Well, all right. The cleaning supplies are in the locked closet between the bathrooms." I toss him the keys. "Hopefully, there's no disaster in there."

He grimaces. "Hopefully."

I push into the restaurant, sighing to see all the debris on the floor. I will have to sweep before I mop.

Glamorous life. At least I come from generations of housecleaners and service workers. I picture Jason in his thousand-dollar jeans, kneeling over a toilet, and burst into giggles.

I'm sort of a wreck.

By the time I empty the mop water and collapse onto the chair in my office, I wonder if I have enough energy to get to my car. I've secured a cleaning company temporarily, so at least I won't have to do this again tomorrow.

But now I need to get home. Leah is expecting me to bring home a pizza for our Friday-night tradition, and I need to order that and pick it up. Mom will undoubtedly take off with friends. She does most weekend nights.

I'm scrolling through my phone looking for the number to Leah's favorite pizza place when I hear a thud behind me.

I whirl around in the chair. Jason empties a bucket in the sink.

"You're just now done?" I assumed he left a long time ago.

"What I'm missing in speed, I make up in thoroughness," he says. "You can brush your teeth in the toilet water."

"Gross."

"Those toilets are no longer gross!"

I shake my head. He seems stupidly proud of himself. He shoves the bucket under the sink and begins a thorough scrub-down. He suds up to his elbows and uses the sprayer to rinse. Poor thing. He's probably never been that up close and personal with a public toilet.

Or any toilet.

But he seems ridiculously chipper about it.

I cross over to the linen shelves and grab a clean towel. "You need something fresh to dry off with so you can begin to rid your body of where you've been."

"Thanks." He accepts the towel and dries off his arms and face and neck. "I'm looking forward to getting rid of this shirt and putting on something clean." He plucks his Antone's T-shirt from his chest. It's streaked and damp.

"I can help you with that." I head to a cabinet in the back corner near Bertha. Inside is a short stack of the old Austin Pickle deli shirts the staff used to wear before we had the huge turnover. We only have a few left, and I didn't know where to order more, so we stopped wearing them.

I toss one to him.

He catches it and flicks it open.

"I wondered if we had these." Then he snaps his mouth shut like he cussed in front of the pope. Interesting.

"I can try to track down where they came from, and where the graphic is. I forgot about them. Although we probably shouldn't order more until I have the budget under control."

"Good thinking," he says. He sets the shirt on the cutting table. "Do you mind if I switch?"

I shake my head.

He pulls his damp T-shirt over his head in one fluid motion.

I should look away, but there's no way I'm going to miss the show. Employee or not.

His shoulders are strong, and his arms thick with muscle. His chest is honed and smooth. My eyes trace the line down his abs to his belly.

Heat flashes through me. This boy works out. My mouth feels hot and dry.

He balls up the shirt and drops it to the floor. "Don't want to set that on our sterile workspace," he says with a grin.

I can't even smile in return. I'm mesmerized by the shift of muscles as he picks up the Pickle shirt and pulls it on. As the fabric drops over his body, I finally drag my gaze away.

My mouth speaks before my brain can stop it, asking, "So I guess you work out?"

He tugs the bottom of the shirt in place and fixes his gaze on me. "Why Miss Strong, were you ogling me while I changed shirts? Should I speak to HR about it?"

My face flames so hot that his infectious grin lights up. "I'm kidding, Nova. Thanks for the shirt."

He seems pretty pleased with himself, though. Figures. A guy like him probably expects women to fawn over him.

Not this girl.

I back away until my butt bumps up against the mixing table. "I'm running late, so we need to go."

Jason scoops up the old shirt. "Have a hot date tonight?"

"Maybe I do."

The way his face falls at my answer, though, sets off a funny tickle in my belly.

"Good. Good." He looks like he's about to say something else, but simply says, "Good," a third time.

"Glad you think so."

"You might want to clean up first, though," he says.

I clap my hands to my face. "What? Do I have something on me?"

He reaches out to touch my cheek. "Maybe a little something right here."

If I thought the way we touched before caused a spark, that was nothing compared to what happens this time. Jason Packwood pours on pure charm, his grin aimed right at my heart.

After all the mornings baking bread, the gazes I caught from him, and then, of course, this recent display of his perfect body, our connection is more like a bomb exploding.

I sidestep away from the table. "Thanks for the help today. I've gotta run."

"Can I walk you to your car?"

For some crazy reason, my head fills with the torrid vision of us in the deserted downtown parking garage, him slamming me against the side of my car, my knees locked around his waist, our mouths fiery in a heated kiss.

I'm still seeing it when I say, "No. I'm fine. See you tomorrow."

I hurry to my office and pretend to mess with my phone. I don't relax until I hear the back door open and close.

He's gone.

What's going on? With him? With me?

This is a complication I don't need.

15

JACE

Everything in my life is upside down.

I used to stay out late, dine at fine restaurants, hang out with beautiful, wealthy, well-connected movers and shakers in society. I partied hard, slept late, and drank only the best tequila.

Now it's a Friday night, I'm wearing a T-shirt featuring a dancing pickle, and watching some long-haired dude in a hot tub on Netflix because Nova told me she liked the show.

While she's on a date with someone else.

Damn.

What the hell am I doing? I keep flirting with her even though I know I shouldn't. Lately, my brain has been consumed with images of her half naked on the mixing table, her knees spread.

That can't be sanitary.

Now, see, that sort of thinking is making me crazy.

Sex and *sanitary* do not go in the same sentence.

I press the heels of my hands to my eyes. I'm exhausted. Frustrated. I need to blow off some steam.

In fact, I do need a shower. I smell like a walking deli.

Among other things.

I remember what I was doing just a couple of hours ago, elbow deep in toilet water, and have to shove that thought away. Nobody can know about that. Nobody.

The next episode of the show rolls around, but I pause the streaming to stand up and stretch. This is not how I expected to spend the year I turned thirty. Alone in my condo after scrubbing a bathroom.

While the only woman I'm interested in goes out with someone else.

My phone buzzes. I bend down to the coffee table to glance at it.

Great. Max.

I'm tempted to ignore it, but truth be told, I could use some thoughts on my next move. So I pick up the call.

"Jace? It's a Friday night! Why is it so quiet?"

Shit. If he spreads the word to the rest of the family that I've become a homebody, I will never live it down.

"I'm in the bathroom of the club."

I hit play on the television and crank the volume. When the noise fills the room, I shout into the phone, "Every time they open the door, it's too loud. Hold on, let me go outside."

I gradually turn down the volume, then slam the front door.

"That's better," I say.

There's silence for a moment on the other end.

"You still there, Max?" I ask.

"Jace, my brother. That noise was episode three of the Witcher. Are you at home watching Netflix by yourself on a Friday night?"

Shit.

"Was there a reason for this call?" I'm not going to give Max the satisfaction of saying he's right.

"I wanted to check in with you, bro. You've gone radio silent on everybody, and you have a situation down there. Did you figure out where you were bleeding money?"

"Not yet. But Nova's working on it. I tried going in to look at the books when the deli was closed, but she was working and nearly busted me."

"I don't think it's her."

"You're judging her based on one phone call?"

"Not completely. If you had your head out of your ass, you'd know the accountant has been monitoring our accounts closely for this challenge. So, unlike the aggregate statements we got a month ago, we can all see what every brother is doing in terms of sales, expenses, profits and losses."

"Dude. That's all Greek to me."

"Right. You got a degree in Humanities or some bullshit."

"The study of humans is important, asshole."

"Yeah, I know exactly how you like to examine humans, particularly the female variety. But that's not the point. You're a smart guy. You can figure it out. It's numbers. Red ones go out. Green ones go in. Make sure there are more green ones than red ones."

"Thanks for the kindergarten lesson." I plunk down onto my sofa. "Obviously you looked. So, give it to me. What did you see?"

He chuckles. "You're doing better. Your weekday sales kick both mine and Anthony's butts. It's probably your downtown location. We make up for it on the weekends."

I sit up. "Should I open more on the weekends?"

"Dunno. Ask your manager. But weekdays are your jam. And you're going up."

"Nova hasn't said anything about more business."

"Well, your profits are increasing. A couple thou a week. That's all I can tell you. Unlocking why means a deep dive into your numbers."

I stand up and start pacing the room. "Do they separate the cash versus credit transactions in the report?"

"Not that I can see. Why?"

"Just a theory. Is there any way to separate those? Can I call the accountant and ask them to do that for me?"

"Probably. The cash should be deposited manually by your manager, or somebody she appoints to do it. You think something's up?"

Susan's gone. She's been gone. She can't steal cash from the safe if she isn't there. And if Nova wasn't keeping track of it from register to bank, then it would be her fault.

Damn. I don't know.

"What's turning in your head, Jace?"

"I'll let you know if it pans out to anything."

"You can always put Audra on it," Max says. "She's got more brains than the three of us put together."

"Good idea. Thanks."

Max chuckles. "Don't stay up too late Netflix and chilling with yourself."

"You can shut the hell up."

He keeps laughing, so I kill the call. Brothers. Assholes.

But he did have a point about the books. And I need to know more about the cash transactions going in and out of my deli. If Susan's been gone six months, the only reason they'd increase since I've been there would because—I'm there. Watching.

I drop back onto the sofa, my head in my hands. I refuse to believe Nova has anything to do with the losses. But the fact is, once I arrived at the deli, it stopped happening. Maybe my presence got in somebody's way. It could be Lamonte. Or Kate or Elda or Arush. Who knows? Maybe even the cleaning crew got access to the safe.

But I do know one thing for sure. I need Audra to pinpoint the exact moment when profit started to rise and if it was cash-related.

And second, I need to get Nova to move me up to working the register so I can see for myself.

I t's six a.m. and Mom is not home.

I jerk a brush through my hair, my eye on the phone screen. I've texted her three times. I have to arrive at work at seven to start the bread. No one can do this for me.

Leah and I were up late last night watching old episodes of *I Love Lucy*. So my baby sister is still crashed in her bed, and I can't leave her alone.

I pull on a pair of distressed jeans and a green hoodie. Austin is being Austin today and dropped from warm and pleasant yesterday to freezing this morning. The cold is not improving my mood. Low-end apartments don't come with smart thermostats, so our place got chilly before I woke up this morning and cranked the heat.

I stand below the vent, letting the warm air blow my hair back.

My phone buzzes with the alarm that I have to start driving in fifteen minutes to make it.

Dang it. Mom? Where are you?

Back in the days when Susan opened the deli, it didn't matter if I wound up late. My pay got docked, but that was the only consequence.

Now I'm in charge, and the schedule is all on me. I wait five more minutes, and then I have no choice. Even if Mom does reply at this point, she can't get home in time for me to make the drive.

I pop into Leah's bedroom, dim and softly pink from the unicorn nightlight near her bed.

I gently shake her awake. "Leah, baby, I'm so sorry. I have to take you to work with me. Mom's not here."

Leah sits up in a rush. "Where is she? What happened?"

"I think she was out late with her friends. Don't worry. But I need you to get ready."

"Can't I stay here by myself?"

"Not yet. Maybe when you're twelve. But not in fourth grade."

Leah whines a little more, but she doesn't argue. I pull a pair of jeans and a sweatshirt from her drawer and pass it to her. "I'll make you some breakfast at the deli."

"Can I have cheesecake?" Her eyes light up, seeing a loophole she can exploit.

"Eggs first, and then you can have cheesecake."

"Yes!" She pumps her fist.

"Now hurry. We have to leave in five minutes."

Leah scrambles out of bed with her clothes and rushes to the bathroom.

Still no message from Mom. She's been doing better

since we got our own place. Regular food, a schedule, and neighbors who notice if she stumbles in at three in the morning, all work together to tone down her behavior.

I thought we had gotten a chance to start over, even if at the expense of my student loans.

Maybe this is just a blip. Maybe she really is hurt somewhere.

My belly quivers for a moment, imagining my mom bleeding in an alley. But hadn't she said she was going over to see Rose? They were going to make drinks. So, no, she was passed out on the sofa there. And I have to deal with the fallout.

Leah emerges and we dash around the living room for a moment, looking for her shoes. Then we're finally outdoors, starting up my ancient Ford Focus and headed toward the deli.

Leah's had the foresight to grab her backpack, and she pulls out a notepad to draw pictures of unicorns and emojis, her two favorite things.

"Do you think Mom is passed out drunk somewhere?" she asks.

I suck in a breath. "What do you know about that?"

"I know she hides bottles in the cabinet over the refrigerator. She has to get the ladder out to get them down."

Actually, I'm the one who hides my mother's bottles up there, a fact that makes her very upset.

"I think she went over to her friend Rose's and got tired."

"She should've set an alarm."

"You're exactly right." I reach over and tug on her ear, which makes her giggle. "I pulled the switch, now you have to tell me a joke." It's an old shtick of ours.

Leah scrunches her nose while she tries to think of one. Her hair is pretty crazy, still a snarl of long brown strands. But her cheeks are rosy and her eyes happy. She's more of a morning person than I am.

"Okay. How do you get a squirrel to like you?"

"I don't know."

"Act like a nut!"

"That's a good one!"

"I read it in a book."

"Nice job remembering it."

The drive is mercifully easy this early on a Saturday morning. I wonder if I can convince Jace Pickle to appoint an assistant manager to help, so I don't have to be the first one there every day. Probably not. It's not like we're open late. The deli only serves through lunch and we close by mid-afternoon every day.

The hours aren't unacceptably long, even as a manager, and I am guaranteed Sundays off since we're not open. I'm getting paid to do this. And after my income increased, I secretly opened a second bank account my mother doesn't know about. I only put the old amount I earned into the previous one.

I love her, but I'm not stupid.

I pull into my usual parking garage a couple of blocks down.

"Why don't you park in front of the deli?" Leah whines. "There are spaces and nobody's in them."

"Those should go to the customers," I say. "I'm here all day, but they go in and out."

"But now we have to walk. It's cold."

"It's not that cold."

The two of us huddle as we scurry down the block. I unlock the back door, relaxing at the warmth inside. In the height of summer, when temperatures can exceed a hundred degrees for weeks on end, we sometimes have trouble keeping the kitchen cool while baking the bread. But now, firing up the proofing oven, I'm glad for the warmth.

I open my office so Leah can spin in my chair.

Then I head to Mr. Chill to grab some eggs and a jug of milk. I need butter, but there aren't any loose blocks, so I have to pause to break open a new crate.

When I walk out of the fridge, I hear voices.

I recognize Jason's laugh. "That's a good one! You got any more where that came from?"

Now Leah. "What kind of tree fits in your hand?"

"I don't know!"

"A palm tree!"

"Love that one, too!"

I plunk my ingredients on the mixing table and walk over to the office.

Jason leans against the wall while Leah gazes up at him with stars in her eyes. "Jason likes my jokes," she tells me.

"I bet he does."

"Do you like *I Love Lucy*?" Leah asks Jason. "Because last night, Nova and I watched three hours straight while we were eating pizza."

Jason grins at me. "Oh, did you? Sounds like you had a pretty great *date*."

Busted.

"My mom didn't come home last night so that's why I'm here," Leah says. "Sometimes she gets too many bottles down from over the fridge and doesn't come home."

Oh, geez. "Okay, Leah, why don't you get back to your drawing? Jason and I need to make the bread."

I hustle back to the table. My face feels like fire.

"*I Love Lucy*," he says. "Sounds like a smashing Friday night."

"Hush." I crack the eggs with too much force and the shell shatters into the bowl.

Jason peers in. "I believe you just showed that egg who's boss."

"Don't you have bread to make?"

"I do, I do. It's almost the end of March. Do we have a special bread for April?"

I head toward the stove. "The bread isn't like the pickle of the month with a definitive beginning and end. We run the specials for as long as they are doing well."

"Everybody loves my bread," Jason says.

Leah materializes next to him. "What bread is that?"

"It's called Dill—"

"It's pickle bread," I say quickly and flash Jason a murderous look. "It's the white bread we normally have with pickle bits in it."

"Can I help?" Leah asks.

"Yes," Jason says.

"No," I say.

Jason and I look at each other.

Leah laughs. "You guys are silly." She looks up at Jason with soft, gooey eyes. "I know how to use measuring cups."

"Excellent," Jason says. "I sometimes have trouble with measuring cups, and I could use the help."

I roll my eyes and turn back to the eggs. But even as I dump them in the pan with more force than necessary, my heart thuds. Leah's never had a male figure in her life. In fact, we don't know who her father is.

I've kept any men I've dated far, far away. Leah attaches easily to adult men. It's clearly a longing she has. I've protected her. There's no sense breaking both of our hearts when one leaves.

And now there's Jason.

When I turn around with the finished eggs, Jason has gotten a stool for Leah, and the two of them are sifting flour.

"Eat your eggs, Leah," I say. "You have to do it away from the bread. We can't have your germs."

"Jason gave me gloves." She wiggles her plastic-covered fingers.

"That's great. We'll get you a new pair after you eat."

"Aww." She tugs on Jason's shirt. "Nova promised me cheesecake after I eat my eggs. Do you like cheesecake?"

"I do," he says. "My grandma makes the best cheesecake in the world."

"Better than the ones here?"

"Exactly the same," he says.

That's interesting. He's been using his grandmother's techniques for the bread, and now admits the cheese-cake is the same. Maybe he's a closer friend of the Pickle family than he's let on. A cousin? An illegitimate cousin? Now that would be interesting.

Maybe I'll look him up. I finally got Internet service, and more importantly, Netflix, after my raise. I could fire up the ancient laptop I used to use for school and type in his name.

I should have done this before.

Leah scoots to the end of the table, away from where Jason continues to make the bread. I move around the kitchen, grabbing more bowls and the pans for the proofing oven. But I watch the two of them from the corner of my eye.

I'm going to find out more about Jason Packwood.

My sister is smitten.

And if I'm willing to admit it, I have to say one thing.

So am I.

Mom finally shows up around noon to grab Leah. It's the middle of the lunch rush, and I'm short Kate, who had a wedding to attend.

I gesture her toward the back and try to keep the line moving.

Jason arrives to refill the pepper jack and provolone. "You should teach me the register," he says. "Maybe when it slows down, I can handle the last few of the day.

That way, I could be of more use when things get crazy."

I nod at him. He's learned most everything else the employees do. He can make all of the dishes, including the tricky stuffed pickles. He bakes the bread. Sets up and empties the sandwich line. Even cleans the bathrooms. Pretty much the only things he doesn't know yet are running the register and balancing the receipts.

By the time the line goes down, Mom and Leah are gone. I go over the conversation I'll have with her when I get off work. It's seriously not fun to have to be the parent to your mother.

Lamonte starts reducing the amount of meat and cheese on the sandwich line so we don't have too much sitting out when the customer flow drops. As he walks by with the stack of metal bins, he bumps my shoulder. "What's stuck in your craw?"

"Mom was out all night. I had to bring Leah."

"Oh. That woman." Lamonte knows all about my issues with my mother. "She has seriously got to grow up." He heads to the back.

Jason passes him and holds the door. "Is it a good time to go over the register?" he asks me.

I glance over the deli. Only three tables are filled, and no one is in line.

"Sure."

I show him the ordering system, and how to key in the sandwiches, drinks, desserts, and extras. "There are two coupons on the national website. Here's how you put that discount in."

"We have coupons?" He seems surprised.

"Sure. The website is maintained by the chain."

"Huh."

We practice an order, and then I cancel it out. The cash tray slides open and I bump it closed.

"Is there a way to open this if you accidentally close it when you're trying to give change?" Jason asks.

"Yes, you have to key in a certain sequence."

I show him how it works, and the tray opens again.

"How do we make sure we have enough change?"

"I keep a fair amount in the safe," I tell him. "If the stack of twenties gets too high, lift the bottom tray and shove them underneath. I rarely have to do a refill run, because I'm solid on what we need. But every once in a while, something strange happens, like a bus full of kids who all have twenty-dollar bills. That will require opening the safe for more small bills."

"Are you the only person who can get into the safe?"

"Currently. We should probably assign someone else in case I get hit by a bus."

"Hit by a bus? That's cheerful."

"It's a business thing. Every company should have a plan for what they would do if the most important player is hit by a bus. Could the doors be unlocked? Could they operate the business? Take money? Or would everything fall apart? It's the best test." I lean on the counter. "Didn't you learn this in business school? It's a 101 sort of topic."

"Oh right, yeah. I remember. But right now, if you were hit by a bus, Austin Pickle would fall apart."

I shrug. "I guess Jace Pickle would have to come down here and handle it."

"When Susan was manager, did we pass the bus test?"

"I don't know. It was a different crew then. I seem to recall an assistant manager type person who filled in for her. But I was a part-timer then."

"So, you went from part-timer to running this place?"

I shove the register closed. "Not right away. We had some other crew in the middle. I was able to work full-time over the Christmas holiday, and then it all happened."

It was a hot mess, but we made it through.

An elderly couple walks through the door. "You want to try?" I ask him.

"Sure," he says. "They don't look too scary."

Jason stands with me as we take the couple's order, and I make the sandwiches.

When we head to the register, I watch him go through the process of ringing it up and accepting the credit card.

When the couple has settled down to eat, I tell them, "Perfect. You learn quickly." I glance at the clock. "Only fifteen minutes till closing time. Can you go check on the back and see what the dish status is?"

He nods and heads out. I watch him push through the door, and his butt definitely looks good in those jeans. I remember the moment when he took off his shirt, and all the intense daydreams I've had since then.

The way he worked with my sister this morning hasn't hurt anything.

He seems trustworthy and smart. He picked up this new skill easily.

He's willing to come in early. He's pulling as many hours as me these days. And he doesn't seem like he's going anywhere anytime soon.

Maybe I ought to reel him in.

JACE

I absolutely do not expect the message that comes through on my iPad late Sunday morning.

Reviewing books later today. Want to come?

I fall back onto my bed, shocked.

Nova can't be that impressed with my cash register skills.

But maybe something's started to give.

I lie there a full five minutes, my head whirling with possibility, when I realize I haven't written her back.

I quickly tap out a message: *Absolutely. What time?*

Nova provides a time about two hours away.

I head to the bathroom for a shower and a pep talk. This is the first real opportunity I've had to be alone with her. No crew is going to come in and interrupt us. There will be no demands pressing on us to get the morning duties done.

Maybe we'll even solve the mystery of the accounting problems once and for all.

Then perhaps I can confess who I am and get this

secret off my back. I don't know how Nova will react. She's unpredictable, which is exactly what makes her so intriguing.

When I arrive at Austin Pickle, the back door is unlocked. I hold my hand on the lever for a moment, my belly tense.

This is nuts.

I'm never nervous around women.

Around me, spring has sprung. The cold has blown out, and the afternoon is bright and warm. It's the type of day poets write about. Sunshine and birdsong.

And I'm meeting Nova, alone.

I push inside the kitchen. The big, open room is dim, only the bright light from Nova's office spilling out.

"I would like to try your pickles, please!" I call out, then inwardly grimace. I haven't said anything that dorky since sixth grade.

"No pickles for you!" she calls.

Okay, that makes me laugh.

Nova appears in the doorway of her office, the light behind her spilling around her.

And my breath catches.

Gone are the camo pants and army boots.

Cutoff jeans reveal an endlessly perfect expanse of thigh, the ragged edge taunting me as the bits of string caress her skin. Just below the knee, well-worn leather cowboy boots elongate her legs. Her signature tank top is siren red and has only the barest spaghetti straps.

Which means she can't possibly be wearing a bra.

While I'm staring to find out, she either catches a chill or knows I'm looking. Her nipples pucker.

And I have my answer.

The back of my neck prickles as I will my dick to stay in control.

Nova turns away. "If you're done gawking, I thought you might be interested in these printouts."

I can barely hear her words. Now that she's walking away, all I can think about is that perfect ass neatly filling out the decorated pockets of her jean shorts. Her long brown hair is in its usual ponytail, but loose and low, silky strands flowing down her back

Since her back's to me, I quickly make an adjustment to make my half-mast status a little less obvious.

What the hell is going on? I'm normally an iron will of control.

But if this is how Nova Strong dresses on a warm Austin day, cancel my ticket, because I'm never going back north.

She plunks down into her office chair, and I can't do anything but admire the bobble her breasts make as she lands.

I'm obsessed with the idea of sliding that tiny strap off her shoulder and baring the puckered nipple for my mouth.

"Jason? Are you still with us?"

Shit. My gaze makes it up to her face. It's the same as always, only a touch of mascara and lip gloss. I'm not sure she even needs that. She's the most beautiful thing I've seen in my life.

"Are you okay?" she asks.

"Yes. Of course." I clamber for something to say. "It got warm out, didn't it?"

She gives me an expression of *What the hell?* Then glances down at her shorts.

"Yes, I got the chance to wear my favorites again. Plus, it's not a workday." She kicks up her leg to show off the boots, and the way her thigh muscle flexes makes me salivate.

I'm a goner. Hook, line, and sinker. Nova Strong can ask me for anything and it's all hers.

After a hard gulp, I finally manage to say, "Nice boots."

"I got them at a thrift shop two years ago. They're surprisingly comfortable."

"Are they?" I'm aware I'm not making charming conversation, but I'm barely holding it together.

She cocks her head at me, then shrugs. "All right, the numbers. Have a seat." She pushes a folding chair toward me with her boot and gestures to the pages spread out on the desk. That's when I spot a pair of glasses lying on a page. Red, like her shirt. Shaped like hearts.

"What are those?" I ask as I sit down. But I'm already dying, literally on fire, to see her put them on.

"Just reading glasses."

I can barely eke out the words, but manage to say, "Are you going to put them on?"

Her lips purse as she considers my question. I'm pretty sure she's on to me, but I'm so far gone I don't care. "I think I can read these pages without them. The type's not too bad."

I can't handle it. I have to set aside all pride, all manliness, all pretenses. "I would like to see them on you."

She laughs with a shrug of her shoulders that draws my attention to the red straps again.

I'm so fucked.

"Jason, you're strange. Do you have a librarian fantasy or something?"

Mostly a Nova fantasy, but I can't say that. "Maybe."

She picks them up and takes her time unfolding each arm on the frame.

Yeah, she's on to me.

When she slides them on her face, there is no hiding my reaction. I'm full mast. All the way.

I snatch up a file folder and I drop it in my lap. My voice barely works, but I manage to squeak out, "Let's look at numbers."

Okay, I'll confess.

I wore this outfit on purpose.

It's not something I wear often. But back when I was in college and went on dates, I would sometimes pull this one out to have a bit of fun. Especially if the guy wasn't Texas born and raised. Those boys harbor all these ridiculous stereotypical fantasies about Texas girls in short shorts and cowboy boots. Daisy Duke made the look famous in the 80s, and celebrities like Jessica Simpson have perpetuated it.

I did skip the stalk of hay between my teeth.

It's not a look I'm entirely comfortable with. It's a lot of leg. And sitting on this office chair makes me self-conscious about my thighs.

But watching Jason Packwood squirm is worth it. Every bit.

I hope he doesn't think he's hiding what's going on in his pants. That file folder is not resting comfortably on his lap.

Packwood.

I have to suppress my crazy urge to giggle.

I shift the glasses on my nose. I do need them at times. I made the mistake, when I picked them out, of taking my little sister with me. Since I rarely use them, I saw no harm in indulging her in the laugh of choosing the heart-shaped ones.

They're not real glasses, of course. Just magnifiers. You can get all sorts of crazy shapes in those.

Regardless, now that I know Jason is a normal human and not wielding the supercharged willpower of a rich boy who never thinks about slumming it, I'm ready to get to business.

My ego is assuaged.

Mission accomplished.

When I'm sure he remembers my eyes are up *here*, I say, "Okay, I found some stuff. It seems right before Susan left, she changed several procedures involving billing, delivery confirmations, and deposits."

Jason visibly shakes himself, like he's coming out of a stupor, and leans forward to look at the notes. "These are emails," he says.

"Right. These are her requesting a change to electronic billing and paperless delivery confirmation. Not every vendor has that sort of system in place, but she changed what she could."

Jason looks back up in my face, and his jaw tightens. I pull off the glasses. I have a feeling we'll get more accomplished without the distraction.

"But doesn't it make sense for her to do that if she's going on medical leave?" Jason asks.

"Yes, except her alleged medical problem came on, and I quote, 'suddenly and unexpectedly, requiring immediate lifestyle changes.' But the changes were done weeks ahead of her saying that." I push another email toward him. This one is between Susan and the owner, Jace Pickle.

Jason snatches it up to look closer. "This went directly to—" he hesitates. "To the owner. Did he ever receive it?"

I shrug. "I don't see why he wouldn't. But Jace has not been very involved in his business. Maybe it got buried in a deluge of unread messages."

Jason shifts in his chair, moving the file folder from his lap to the desk. "What all did she change before she left? And which parts didn't make sense?"

"We get a ton of desserts from the New York branch. Someone up there directly supervises the making of the cheesecakes and tortes and ships them down."

"Grammy Alma," Jason says.

Wait. "Your Grammy?" I ask. I distinctly remember Jason calling his bread and cheesecake making grandmother Grammy.

He shakes his head. "Sorry. Alma..." He stops again. "Alma Pickle. She's like the grandmother of the chain."

I'm not going to let him get away with the slip-up. "But you also call her Grammy?"

Jason revives that snake oil smile I remember from the day we met. I haven't seen it in a while, and I immediately go on guard.

"She's a mother figure to me. She taught me how to make a lot of things in the Pickle deli. I am a close part of the family."

He chose his words carefully, but my suspicion remains. Something here's not right. I spin the heart glasses on the desk, trying to come up with a way to get at the truth.

"You know, I find it interesting you wanted to work at this particular deli. I'd think you would get a lot out of working at the Manhattan Pickle with the founder. He's got tons of experience running that gigantic restaurant. Here, you're learning from someone who has to fake it all the time."

He holds my gaze. "You don't look like you're faking."

I search his face for his intention with that double entendre, but he's back to the Jason I know, handsome and attentive and thoughtful.

"Well, I am. I might have two years of business school behind me, but it's nothing next to you and your MBA."

"Right. Let's just say New York isn't my scene. I needed to get away."

Interesting. Maybe he went through a bad breakup. Or his family was hounding him. Maybe he would admit that to me one day. When we were more personal.

My shoulders relax.

He pushes aside the emails to lift one of the spreadsheets. "So, what is this about, the cheesecakes?"

"They're stacked up like crazy in the freezer. It hasn't made any sense. I remember us selling them before, but not in the numbers we're receiving. And corporate hasn't given us any specials to offload them. Big portions of rich desserts don't really go hand-in-hand with a lunchtime deli. So I started looking into it."

I lean in and point to a line on the spreadsheet. "This is when Susan left. And a couple of weeks before, she started ordering the cheesecakes in greater numbers."

"Why would she do that?"

"I think it might be because this delivery is handled differently monetarily." I put another printout in front of him. "Look here. With that bigger delivery, she can show that we got, say, five hundred dollars' worth of the cheesecakes in and put it inside the system as deliveries received. But we don't have to pay out the money, because the deliveries between delis aren't billed, but credited to the chain."

He nods. "But she still entered it as a payment upon delivery. That way she can make it look as though we paid out more money for deliveries than we did, so that she can hide money that's actually going somewhere else."

"Exactly."

"But where is that money going?"

"I'm still looking, but I suspect the cash deposits. The credit card transactions go straight to national for accounting."

"But not the cash," Jason says.

"Exactly. The big bills used to go to the bank via courier. Everything is well documented." I open the folder he had on his lap and show the receipts.

"But then what happened?"

"She canceled courier service and started making the delivery runs."

"So she could pull cash without anyone noticing in between?" Jason asks. "But she's not here anymore. She hasn't been here to pull cash for six months."

I hand him another printout. "I know. But look at these cash deposits. Once she starts the manual deposits, they sharply drop until they hit a very specific number, one that's less than average."

Jason looks up at me. "Five hundred dollars?"

"Bingo."

"She was taking five hundred dollars a day from the deli?"

"Precisely."

Jason's ears have turned red. Wow. He's really upset.

"No wonder this deli is nearly bankrupt," he says.

Wait, what? "The deli's bankrupt? Jace Pickle said nothing about the deli being in trouble."

Jason stares at the page a moment longer. "Not yet. But I'll admit this much. One of the reasons I came here was to see if I could turn the ship around." He sets the pages back on the desk. "The family will be so grateful to you for figuring this out. It's been a great mystery."

I push back in my chair, giving me some distance from this guy. Who is he, really? "I don't understand."

"This is Jace Pickle's fault." Jason's mouth turns down into a grimace. "If he'd have paid more attention, he would've seen these changes. I think the family is indebted to you."

"Was this why you sneaked into the office that

time?" Things start to fall into place. How he got in there. And why Jace was so anxious for me to keep him here.

"We weren't sure what we were dealing with down here," Jason says. "But you figured it out."

He's right. I did. "I couldn't have done it if I hadn't been given manager status. I didn't have the access before."

"That was the smartest thing they did," Jason says. "And you're perfect as manager. The crew loves you. This place runs smoothly. Now that we've figured out where we were leaking money, I think the deli will be very successful."

His face is so earnest as he looks at me, I believe every word he says. It's clearly the truth. But my stomach sinks. "Does this mean you're going to leave now?"

Jason fiddles with the papers. "I don't think we're quite done yet. If the money kept going missing after Susan left, she had someone helping her. Someone who could still be on staff."

I nod. "I thought I was going crazy. That I didn't understand something. I—"

Ugh. I hate to admit this.

"What?"

"You might not be so impressed with me after I say this."

"Unlikely."

"Well, on that first day, you know I gave Lamonte money to buy pickles. It took a while before I got everything straightened out and could stop using cash. I had to get on the bank account. Get Audra—Jace Pickle's assistant—to have me authorized to make deposits and deal with the bank."

"Okay. What's wrong with that?"

"Before I could enter expenses myself, I had to keep sticky notes. So, in the last couple of weeks, I've been going crazy trying to balance all the cash."

"You think cash is still going missing?"

"I thought maybe I'd done things and forgotten to write them down. But we're still short cash."

"You think someone is stealing?"

"Yes. It's not the even five hundred like it was before. I guess when you fired Susan, she got cut off from however she was getting it."

"But it's still going missing?"

I nod. "I can change procedure. I could make a deposit every day after I take it from the register. To ensure no one's getting in here."

Jason nods. "That sounds like a good plan eventually. But right now, we want to keep everything the same, so they won't know we're on to them. Maybe set up a security camera."

"That could catch them."

"But anyone can get into the register."

I suck in a breath. "Do you think I'm part of this?"

Jason reaches out to lay his hand on my arm. "No. I don't think that at all. In fact, I think you're the only reason the ship has held together all these months."

I relax against the chair. Jason withdraws his hand, and my heart hammers painfully. I liked it there.

He stands. "Maybe we should check the safe. See if there's anything obvious. Where is it?"

"It's hidden in a cabinet in the kitchen. Being one of the cash register operators, I had access to it even before Susan took off. Sometimes we need change in the middle of the day."

I snatch up my keys and we head into the kitchen. It's dim, and also quiet; so different from normal working hours. I flip on the overhead, and the stainless-steel shines in the brightness.

"Over here." I lead him to the corner and shove a key into a wood cabinet.

Inside are shelves stacked with customer T-shirts and hoodies with the Pickle logo. People can buy them as souvenirs. One says, "I'm apparently a really big dill." Another one says, "I'm done dillin' with you."

Beneath them lies a false drawer. When I unlock it, the front facade swings open.

The metal safe fills the space. I quickly dial in the combination and pull open the door. Inside, the cash from this week is exactly where I left it in its locked zipper bag.

"Should we count it?" I ask. "It's lying exactly the way I left it."

"I don't think that's necessary," Jason says. "We'll eventually want to change the combination, though."

"I agree. If Susan left her key and the combination, anybody could be getting in here."

"I'd like to see the desserts," Jason says. "Are we talking a few extra? A few cases?"

I laugh. "Oh, no. Have you not gone into JP?"

"No. I haven't had any reason to."

"Prepare yourself for sugar overload."

I lock up the cabinet. The walk-in freezer is built in the far corner past the sinks. When I open the heavy steel door, a rush of cold blows the loose tendrils of hair away from my face.

When I turn sideways to step inside, Jason's eyes are on my boobs again.

Headlights. I know. Jason is definitely a nipple man.

"We're going to have to squeeze," I warn him. "It's wall-to-wall desserts in here."

All the shelves inside are packed floor-to-ceiling with crates of cheesecakes, tortes, chocolate cakes, and key lime pies, our signature desserts.

"What the hell," Jason breathes.

I take careful steps to the back of the freezer to avoid bumping my bare legs against the frosty crates. There's only a narrow aisle, about two feet wide, between the boxes stacked in front of the shelves. They reach shoulder-high. Thankfully, I stopped the deliveries before our game of cheesecake Tetris reached all the way to the door.

Jason follows me in. The room dims as the door clicks closed. Only a bare bulb illuminates the space, the light mostly blocked by boxes.

"We won't get locked in?"

"No, it opens from the inside."

He glances around. "This looks like a year's worth of desserts."

"Exactly."

"What are you gonna do with all these?"

I shrug. "Some probably need to be tossed. I've been thinking about some specials, but honestly, between trying to figure out these books, and certain annoying unpaid employees who need training, I haven't had time to come up with anything."

He steps closer. "I'm annoying?"

We're only a foot apart. My temperature has already fallen in the cold and I shiver. "You have to admit, you were pretty terrible at first."

"And now?"

I cross my arms in front of my belly. "I can 'dill' with you."

He laughs. "Did you just make a pickle pun?"

"It wasn't kosher?"

"Only if you're gherkin my chain."

Our laughter echoes off the boxes. My arms are cold, but inside I'm radiating heat that stops my shivers. Jason has never been this close.

But I want him closer. I want to kiss him. He's probably going to leave now that we've figured things out, and I don't want him to go without knowing what his lips feel like.

"I think you're cold," he says.

My throat catches. "I am, a little."

"Should we head out, or..."

"Or?" I hold his gaze. "Maybe I might *relish* a little warmth."

That's enough for him. Jason comes at me like a jaguar on prey. His arms draw me close, and my breasts flatten against his firm chest. His mouth claims mine, and there is no doubt he's wanted this for a while. His kiss is hungry, fervent, and hot.

I unravel my arms from my belly and wrap them around his back. He's the only warm thing in this frozen place.

I'm lost. I'm thrilled. My insides sing.

His tongue slides along my lips, and I take him in greedily. My heart beats not only in my chest, but also in my throat and thickly between my legs.

His hands rove down my back, finding new spots to warm. I can't get enough of him, wanting his body closer, then closer still.

One of the straps of my top fall down my shoulder. Jason groans against my mouth. "I can't resist this." His lips are impossibly warm as he makes his way down my jaw, kissing my collarbone, his tongue sliding along the swell of my breast, pushing the red cotton tank down.

My nipple puckers tightly at the cold, but quickly relaxes, warm with his mouth on me. I clutch at him, dizzy from the cold and the heat at the same time.

This is what I've wanted since that morning we made bread.

It got so much stronger when I saw him with my sister.

And in the euphoria of solving the mystery of the accounting books, I'm finally getting it.

His hand presses my breast up so he can take it more fully into his mouth. I wrap my arm around his head, drawing him close to me. My hip brushes against one of the boxes, covered in frost, and I realize I'm stuck.

"Jason?"

He murmurs against my breast. "Yes?"

"I think I'm attached to one of the boxes."

He pulls away. "What?"

I shift away from the stack, but my red shirt still sticks to the crate.

"I guess I melted the frost," I say with a laugh.

"I'd make a terrible pun, but I just want you in my mouth again."

Desire darts through me like a lightning strike.

"I guess we can take this outside the freezer?" I don't want to stop either. I feel painfully alive, like someone injected a fiery elixir into my veins.

Jason grabs the hem of my shirt and warms it with his hand until it comes away from the box.

"My hero."

He stares at my face. "This is probably a bad idea." But even as he says it, his hand covers my naked breast to protect it from the cold, and I melt into him.

Our lips lock together, the fever not broken, but stronger, hotter.

But he's right. He is my employee.

My heart sinks, and I pull away. "Is it because I'm your boss?"

He goes still. "I don't know." His forehead lands on my shoulder. "Shit."

He lowers his hand. My breast puckers painfully in the sudden cold, so I lift my shirt back to cover it.

Jason steps away, and it's as if my whole body has turned to ice.

"I guess we should probably get out of the freezer," he says.

I have to swallow hard to reply. "Probably."

He leads us out of JP, and I'm careful not to brush any more of the crates.

"I think we should think this through," he says carefully, his eyes looking anywhere but at me.

"Are you going to leave?" I grasp the edge of the mixing table, trying to keep my voice level, but inside, the glow is slowly fading out.

He shakes his head. "I'd like to stay until we catch the crook."

I nod. "I'll try to get exact numbers on how much cash has gone missing."

He nods. "If you want, we can ask Audra. She's great at crunching data."

My head snaps up. "You know Jace Pickle's assistant?"

He hesitates, and my suspicion rises again.

"I'm pretty tight with the Pickles." He grimaces. "I should go."

After the back door opens and shuts, and the kitchen has gone quiet, I sit in my desk chair and pick up the heart glasses. I feel bereft, as if I'd found something wonderful only to have it snatched away.

It's wrong. I am his boss.

Sort of.

He knows this. Is that why he held back?

But Jason can walk away at any time. His closeness to the Pickles means I can't do anything to him.

Surely, we could give this a try.

As I revisit that moment in the freezer, I know I've never felt as intensely as I do for him.

So, for once, I'm going to do absolutely the wrong thing.

It might not last.

It might be a one-off dalliance for him.

But I'm going to do it.

I'm going to make Jason Packwood mine.

19

JACE

I am so incredibly fucked.

On Monday morning, I know I'm supposed to go in at seven, like I have every morning since I started baking bread with Nova.

It's a time I look forward to. Rolling dough. Telling stupid pickle jokes. And laughing with her before the rest of the crew comes in.

But it's six forty-five, and I should be walking out the door of my apartment.

I can't do it.

I just can't. She doesn't know I'm Jace Pickle. That I had my brother talk to her pretending to be me. That Audra is *my* assistant. That every time she writes me it goes to the number on my iPad and not my real phone.

It's all a lie.

Would she have gone into the freezer and melted the frost on the cheesecake box if she had known who I was?

I don't know.

I don't know how to handle this.

I'm in the middle of this terrible angry rant with myself when I realize, I've left the condo.

I'm in my car.

I'm driving.

I've been so in my head that my body has decided *screw this, bozo*, let's get to work.

I park the car and try to figure out what to do. Go in? Call and quit? What do I say to her after yesterday?

I can still feel her body in my hands. I can taste the sweet nub of her nipple in my mouth.

So, here's the real problem.

I want her again. I want her badly. But I can't.

It's unethical.

It's a lie.

Maybe I can come clean. I can tell her I'm Jace Pickle. I'm the asshole. I'm the one who wasn't there for the crew, for the deli, for her.

I start walking toward my deli with a new sense of determination.

That's what I'll do.

I'll tell her and face the music.

If she throws me out, she throws me out.

But if she doesn't…

Maybe we have a shot.

I won't wait for us to start baking the bread. I won't do anything other than walk straight in there and tell Nova Strong I'm Jace. That I have two names. That both of us are me.

And that I think she's incredible and smart, and I

don't think this deli would be any good without her. And I want to take her on a proper date.

And as soon as she's willing, consenting, and dying for me as much as I'm dying for her, I'll strip her naked, throw her on my bed, and ravish her until we collapse from exhaustion.

And then do it again.

I don't realize how fast I'm moving until I'm already at the back door of the kitchen.

I take a deep breath. I'm Jace fucking Pickle, part of the Pickle Deli Dynasty. I can do this.

We're good together. I can show her that. I will do whatever it takes.

I open the door.

Nova is inside, setting out shiny metal bowls on the main work table.

When I step through the door, her hands go still. She doesn't look at me.

Is she upset at me?

I did walk away from her in the freezer.

I have to fix this.

There are so many things I want to be my first line.

That I'm crazy about her.

Crazy *for* her.

That I only walked away because I felt I had to.

But these have been the best weeks of my life.

And I want to stay in Austin.

For her.

But I know I can't say any of those things.

Not yet.

I have to say only these words: *I am Jace Pickle. I own this deli.*

I shove my keys in my pocket and walk slowly across the tile floor to stand next to her.

She's wearing the little black tank top that I noticed on the first day I worked here. I try not to stare at her body, those perfect uplifted breasts, that sweet curve of hips.

They're not mine to look at. Not yet.

Maybe when I say these things, I'll be able to move toward that goal. To have her be mine. To be with me. At least to try.

The silence has gone on too long. She's turning her head to me, a question.

"Jason—"

"Nova—"

The moment is so intense, and our simultaneous starts so forlorn, that neither of us can help it.

We burst out laughing.

We laugh long and hard, like that day with the flour. We laugh until our eyes are wet. It's the best laughter I've ever felt. I know it means we will be okay.

Nova holds her belly. "I can't stop."

I take a deep breath. It's hard to start my speech with this going on.

But I grab her shoulders and force her to stand up and look at me.

"Nova, I have to talk to you."

"Me too."

We stare at each other and the laughter dies completely away. I'm ready to start my confession, but then Nova knocks me backward, her arms around my neck, pulling me down so she can reach my mouth.

And she's kissing me with all the passion and fervor I've ever dreamed of. There's no cool society girl in this woman. She knows what she wants. And she's going for it.

And it's me. I lift her against my body, pulling up her thighs to circle my waist. She locks her legs around me, and I clutch her sweet ass, finally, in my hands.

Her fingers are in my hair, on my shoulders, my back. She clings to me, and I turn so she sits on the mixing table.

Our mouths melt together, sweet and hot. She tastes of coffee and sugar and good mornings. I could revel in those flavors every day for the rest of my life.

Her hair is down, and I sink my hands into those thick, silky locks. I clutch her head and press her tight against me, my tongue reacquainting itself with every sweet part of her mouth.

She grasps the hem of my shirt and pushes it up, her hands sliding along my ribs and chest.

I'm raging, and all thoughts of talking are long gone. Nova pulls the T-shirt over my head and tosses it toward the sinks. Her hands are everywhere, and every place she touches burns with need.

Any stop signs are blown aside by her eagerness and passion. We know the morning routine. There will be no deliveries, no employees, nobody here for at least two hours.

Too long, sweet, delirious hours.

I grab the bottom of her tank top, and in a split second, it also sails across the kitchen.

She wears a bra today. I make quick work of unfastening it and throwing it into the space behind me.

Now her breasts are mine to taste and caress and own.

Her head drops back as I lower down to take one in my mouth, and then the other. She arches to me, a small groan escaping her lips.

It's the sweetest sound in the world.

I move down even farther, feathering kisses along her ribs and dipping my tongue into her belly button.

She wears the green camo pants today, a thick tan belt circling her hips.

I take my time tugging it open, releasing the clasp, and sliding it out of the loops.

If falls to the floor with a clang.

Her hands let go of me to brace herself up on the stainless-steel table.

I unfasten her pants and pull down the zipper, allowing my eyes to skim up her body to take in those glorious breasts, the jut of her beautiful chin, and her serene, blissed-out face.

Her hair falls behind her in a cascade, almost brushing the table.

This is sweeter than I could have possibly imagined.

I jerk open the pants and slide a hand beneath her ass to lift her. I tug the camos down to her knees and slip a hand against the sweet heat between her legs.

Her panties are pale peach, almost the color of her skin, silky and warm.

I slide along the outside, pressing my middle finger into the fold.

She sucks in a breath.

I don't have time to unlace these Army boots, so I jerk the pants to her ankles and spread her knees.

The wispy panties are easy to shove aside. I slide first one, and then two, fingers into her body.

Her back arches and those gorgeous breasts thrust into the air.

I reach up with my free hand to massage first one than the other, as I work her down below.

She writhes against my hand, her belly flexing, her eyes closed.

I feel like a crazy man, shirtless in the kitchen of my own deli, a mostly naked woman grinding against my hand on the mixing table.

But it's the most amazing thing I've ever experienced. Nova is so outrageously alive. She doesn't care about anything but this connection we have.

I'm drowning in her.

I bend down and jerk aside the panties. I lower my head, breathing against the soft pink of her.

Nova lets out a long, heady exhale in anticipation.

And then I'm in, my face pressed tight to her skin, my tongue sliding along her folds. My thumb circles the nub of her clit.

Her body clenches around me, her thighs brushing my ears.

Her hips move with me, and we become one motion, my face and mouth and lips and tongue working in harmony with her thighs and clit and the sweet heat rising in her body.

Her muscles begin to shudder, and I groove with her, giving exactly what she needs, until her voice begins to cry out. "Jason. God. Jason."

I hold onto her, maintaining our fierce connection, my tongue fluttering.

Her body quivers, and she lets out a careening cry. Her breathing slows, and she falls back on the table, her elbow bumping one of the bowls. I catch it before it clatters to the floor.

She stares at the ceiling, her hair falling off the other side of the table. I want to imprint this image of her in my mind, her gorgeous body laid out on stainless steel, her most sensitive parts pressed against my cheek, still slightly trembling.

I want more of her. All of her.

Every day.

I know I have things to tell her.

I know I have a confession to make.

But that will have to wait for another time.

Because right now, there's no way I'm going to put this absolute perfection at risk.

20

NOVA

W orking next to Jason after that morning's moment on the mixing table is pure torture.

I don't know what came over me. Or him.

Everything is so crazy.

Each time we glance at each other, our foolish grins have to be so huge that everybody knows what we've been up to.

And even though I need to finish the bread—and open the register, and tell the crew where to go, and how to set up, and what our goals are for the day—all I can think about is when I can get them all out of here so I can be alone with Jason again.

Because that moment on the mixing table was hot.

And I want more.

Jason and I work side-by-side, prepping pickles for an afternoon order when Lamonte comes into the kitchen with an empty cheese vat. "Look at the two of you stuffing pickles like you were born to do it."

I glance at Jason and catch his side-eye.

I'm so high from this morning, I can't stop my words. "I've been meaning to teach him the art of the perfect pickle placement."

A strangled sound comes from Jason's throat.

Lamonte pauses on his way to the fridge. "You haven't taught him how to do it before now?"

"Nope," I say, flashing hot with mischief. "I was waiting until the right moment, when I knew his pickle work was worthy."

Jason's shoulders shake slightly. He's trying to hold it together. He manages to say, "The salt is almost out," and heads to Bertha.

Lamonte scoots close. "Is it just me or do I sense some real pickle action happening?"

"He's finally been here long enough to tease," I say.

"Hazing," Lamonte says. "I love it. You doing okay?"

"Never better." I keep my eyes on the pickles I'm scooping out to prepare for stuffing. "We haven't had many of these orders lately. I should look into who used to request them and see if we can send out a flier or something to drum up more business."

"Manager-girl on the case!" Lamonte says as Jason emerges from Bertha with a canister of salt. "You tell the Pickles that Nova Strong is gonna make *all* the money for this store!" He heads to Mr. Chill, sing-songing, "Nova's in the house! Nova's got it going on!"

"How long have you two been friends?" Jason asks.

"Since I hired him."

"Is it hard to be personal with them and their boss too?"

"Not yet. I haven't changed how I do things." I slide a pile of prepped pickles aside and scoop the gutted innards into a bowl. "You ready to stuff a pickle?" I ask.

He doesn't answer, so I turn to him.

"Are we talking about these?" he asks, waving his plastic-gloved hand at the pile I've made.

"Nope," I say. "I'm talking about yours. I hope this morning was just the start."

His eyes catch mine. "I've thought about nothing else."

"Good."

Lamonte returns with a refilled vat. "Don't be doing nothing I wouldn't do!"

"Short list," I holler back as he pushes through the doors.

"Did you tell him?" Jason asks.

"No way."

"Will you?"

I arrange the pickles, scooped side up. "Not likely." I don't want to think too hard about this. What Lamonte might say. What the Pickles would think of me banging their protege.

Damn.

"Should we stop?" I ask him. "I'm your boss."

His throat bobs for a moment. "I don't want to." Then he leans in very close. "I'd drag you into the JP if I didn't think we'd get freezer burn."

Kate pops in. "It's slowing down out there. I'm going to run to class."

Jason and I quickly resume our pickle prep.

"Sounds good," I call. "See you tomorrow."

She turns quickly, her ponytail bouncing. Only when the swinging door goes still do I whisper, "Anticipation."

"I'm counting the minutes."

Lamonte's head emerges through the door next. "Boss lady, you have a phone call."

"Got it!" I rip my gloves off.

"I'll be back," I say.

But when I head to my office, Jason follows.

"You coming?" I ask.

We step inside, and Jason closes the door and flips the lock. "No, you are. Can Nova hold off on that luscious little orgasm scream while she's on the phone?"

"Oh, no," I say, but my panties are already damp.

"Oh, yes." His voice is low and throaty.

I turn away from him to pick up the line. Surely, he's joking.

But he did lock the door.

"This is Nova Strong," I say.

The man on the other line has a smoker's voice, rough-edged. "I understand you're the new manager at Austin Pickle."

"I am," I say, my heart speeding up as I realize Jason is kissing the back of my neck. I have my hair up for the workday, and he slides his lips along my skin. I shiver.

"I wanted to talk to you about coffee. We have the finest fair-trade, organic, small-batch coffee beans in distribution. Tell me, do you grind your own beans or get them pre-ground?"

"Uh… I…" Jason's hands slide under my shirt and inside my bra, cupping both breasts. I let out a long sigh. "We don't grind them," I manage to say.

"I like grinding," Jason whispers, rocking his pelvis into my butt. He's *really* erect.

"We can send them ground," the man says. "We deliver on any schedule. Daily, weekly, or twice a month. We like to ensure our grounds are fresh and we roast daily…" The man keeps talking but I can't hear a word he's saying. Jason has unbuckled my belt, and the zipper slides down with a gentle hiss.

His hand slips into my panties, and he curls his fingers up and inside me. He's already learned what makes me tick. I let out a gasp, holding my hand over the bottom of the phone.

His other hand molds itself to a breast, thumb and finger rolling a nipple. His breath is hot on my neck.

God. His hand delves deeper, and I try to concentrate on the voice on the phone, but I'm too lost.

"Can I make you come now?" Jason asks.

"Yes," I say.

"Great!" the man says. "I'll send someone over tomorrow with samples."

I have no idea what I've agreed to, and I can't think about that. Jason's fingers work me faster, tighter, and he rocks against me. His mouth is hot, and my breast zings with his attention. My thighs shake as everything starts to tighten around him.

I clutch the receiver, unsure if the man is still there. Jason presses me close, his hand moving faster, fluttering, circling, working every angle.

I suck in a breath, and everything clenches. The orgasm begins tight and even, then bursts out, flashing through my core. I list forward, dropping the phone to the desk with a clatter. Jason holds on to me, and I bite down any sounds, refusing to make noise, gripping the desk and Jason's strong arm.

When I've stopped trembling, Jason carefully shifts me around and lowers me to my desk chair.

"You all right?"

I nod.

He picks up the phone. "Still there?" he asks then sets the receiver down. "He's gone."

"I think I just ordered coffee," I say.

Jason laughs. "I will be happy to drink your orgasm coffee."

I kick my leg out. "You're terrible."

He kneels in front of me and zips up my pants. "You're delicious. I think we should put this on my task list for every day, say two o'clock, after the lunch rush?"

My head spins thinking about it.

He sits back on his heels, his hands on my knees. "That looks like a yes to me."

I stare at him, this beautiful, put-together man. His gorgeous face, that perfect stubble. His T-shirt stretches across his chest, and his thighs fill out his jeans.

I feel extremely brazen as I say, "Tomorrow, this office. Two o'clock. You. Naked. I'll bring the condom."

Our eyes clash and while I've said this half-jokingly, his gaze is serious as he adds his own demand.

"Bring a whole box."

21

JACE

I'm not sure what the hell I'm doing.

But I'm loving every minute.

The next day, Nova and I glance at the clock every twenty-seven seconds. I spot her doing it. She sees me. At one point she says, "We should have chosen eight a.m."

Except, Lamonte had been there to help with the bread, as he does twice a week. Technically, I'm not needed those days, but like hell am I going to miss one minute with Nova.

The deli settles down earlier than usual and at one-thirty, Kate comes out to say she'd like to leave early if she could. Lamonte and Elda can hold the fort.

When Kate has disappeared again, Nova says to me, "Early break?"

After our two encounters yesterday, I'm pretty sure my dick has grown three sizes from the pressure.

"I'll race you."

I take off running for the office. Nova laughs,

yanking off her gloves and dropping them in the trash can. "You know the rules!"

Yes, I do. Me. Naked.

I have no problem with that.

She heads toward the deli front, no doubt to make a quick appearance before her *dis*appearance. I don't think about what I'm doing, or how crazy it is.

I head into her office and close the door.

And strip.

Man, she can get me good if she wants to. She could set up a web cam. Tell the rest of the staff to meet her in the office.

I check the window. Still covered.

I'm starting to sweat the whole idea when her door opens a crack.

"You indecent?" she whispers. Her eye peers through the opening.

And *schwam*, the cock engages.

"I see you are." Her smile is huge as she slips inside and locks the door.

I'm not shy by any stretch, but when Nova turns around to check me out, I admit I'm anxious to please her.

She tilts her head, a fist under her chin. "Let me see. On a scale from one to ten—"

I don't let her finish, but snatch her body against mine and shut her up with a long, mind-erasing kiss. When she's gasping against me, I pull away and show her what I've done.

Her bra dangles from my fingertips.

She presses her hands to her chest. "How did you do that?"

"Dexterity and determination."

"You're a naughty, naughty intern."

I admit it, her saying it makes my cock even harder.

"Now, sit," she says and pushes me into her desk chair.

I fall onto the cloth seat. She kneels in front of me and takes my dick in both hands. "This needs some attention."

"It's all for you."

Her gaze lifts to me, those long lashes framing two hungry brown eyes. Shit. I'm done for.

Her lips slide over my shaft, and I have to stifle a groan. My head falls back on the chair and I sink into the seat.

She takes her time, using her hands to cup my balls. Her mouth is warm and wet, and she senses what I'm looking for and adjusts her speed. She's got every move in the playbook, and as each part unfolds, tongue and lips and fingers, I have to pull back from my bliss and clamp down my control.

"Condom?" I ask, barely recognizing my own strangled voice.

She takes one more long, lingering lick, then says, "Top drawer."

I jerk it open. There's a whole string.

"Nice." I pull one off the end and set it on the desk.

"So, boss, what are my instructions?"

She peers up at me and squints one eye like she's

thinking. God, she's beautiful. And perfect. Fuck. I'm so doomed.

"You bend me over this desk and fuck me so hard, I forget what day it is."

I give her a salute, then grab the base of her peach shirt and whip it over her head. "None of this," I say, tossing it on my pile of clothes.

I lean down to say hello to my favorite girls, crushing her breasts to my mouth as I take turns on each one. When Nova's breath is fast and rapid, I unfasten her jeans.

"One day I'll have sex with you without Army boots, but today is not that day."

She gives me a smile, half-drunk with lust.

It's my favorite look.

I jerk the jeans down and have to smile at the panties. They're bright yellow with a big smiley face on the ass.

I smack it. "So damn cute. Why are you so fucking cute?"

"The better to tease you," she says.

I give her a long searing kiss than whip her around to face her desk.

"I don't want to get written up for taking too long," I say. "My job is on the line."

"I'll have to fire you if you don't—" She cuts off when my fingers slide inside her.

"How is my performance review coming?"

She breathes heavily. I grasp her head and push her down so her cheek lands on a pile of papers. "You should have cleaned your desk."

"I'll make you do it," she says. "I'll make you do it naked while I watch."

"Damn. You're hard-core." My cock is raging. I let go of her head and pick up the condom. "What else?"

"You'll be here every day to serve me."

I rip open the condom with my teeth. "Every day?"

"Twice on Sunday."

The condom rolls smoothly over my cock. My fingers rub her clit so hard she slams her fist on the desk. "Now, damn it," she says. "Right the hell now."

I jerk her panties to her ankles and knock her thighs wider with my knees. I grab her hair again and I slide inside her in a long, rending thrust.

She claps her hand over her mouth.

"Don't make a sound, boss. They'll be on to us."

Her breathing causes several loose pages to flutter to the floor. She clutches the edge of the desk as I move behind her, holding on to her hips, and rock into her again and again and again. I've found a reserve of control, and I want this to go on forever, to never stop fucking her. This is the height of everything, Nova, our skin, the connection, the heat rising from our bodies.

Her breasts move back and forth, and her muscles shift and tighten. Her hair falls from the ponytail, spilling like dark silk across her spreadsheets.

Fuck, this is good. Better than my deepest, most intense fantasy.

The pressure rises and I reach around to circle that wet clit waiting for me. I've barely grazed it, when her thighs quiver, she gasps, face pressed to the desk, She lets out a long groan.

I unleash, the torrent flowing out of me, my head light, every glory of the world converging as all the tension of the last three days releases.

I hold her tightly against my body, her muscles clenching around me, my cock pulsing inside her. I've never had a fit like this, a woman willing to do anything. A passion like nothing I've ever seen.

I close in over her back and hold her close, my forehead pressed to her neck. We hang on to the moment a bit longer, breathing in and out, and I press a kiss into her hair. I realize I'm about to say something romantic, and this jolts me into reality.

I've fucked her properly now. The whole nine yards.

And she doesn't even know who I am.

I wash over with guilt.

Shit.

"Hey," Nova says, reaching back to wrap a hand around one of my arms. "You okay?"

"Absolutely," I say, forcing myself to pull it together. "You're like a dream girl."

She laughs. "I think you're the dream guy."

I pull away. "I guess I shouldn't put this in the trash. The cleaning crew will talk."

Nova hands me a piece of paper scribbled with random numbers. "Crumple it up in this."

I do as she says and toss it into her trash bucket.

We dress quietly. I look everywhere but her.

How do I fix this?

I can't come clean right here, right now. That would be horrifying for us both.

"So, you available for dinner tonight?" I ask.

She fastens her pants. "You asking me out?"

"Seems like we might want to do something outside of work."

She doesn't say anything else, and I wonder if I'm wrong that she wants more of me. Maybe a bang with an employee, to do the power play, was all she was after.

"I'd like that," she says, finally.

My shoulders relax about a mile.

"Should I pick you up or do you want to meet?"

"How about we meet here? Out front?"

"Okay. Eight?"

She nods.

We dress quickly. The mood has shifted, as if now we're thinking about all the things this could be.

I know I am.

And all the ways I'm going to screw it up.

22

NOVA

I have all afternoon to think about what's happened between me and Jason over the last couple of days.

I feel utterly out of control. Scenes flash through my head. Me on the mixing table. In my office. Twice!

And now we're going on an actual date.

I search through my closet, finding nothing to wear other than thrift-store camo, tank tops, and loose sweatshirts. I'm trying to save my money for school, and I don't have time to shop anyway, so I head to my mom's closet.

She has some new things, courtesy of my school loan.

I find a simple black skirt that should work. I don't know where we're going, but if it's what Jason's used to, it will be nicer than any restaurant I've ever been to.

I search a bit more and find a silky, dark-red button-up blouse. What should go underneath?

I don't own fancy lingerie, but I do have a few lacy

things I deemed too uncomfortable to bother with, so they aren't worn out.

But shoes. I can't exactly wear Army boots with this ensemble. Mom and I aren't the same size.

Didn't I go to a funeral once? I bought a pair of black shoes for that.

I head to my room and lay the skirt and blouse on the bed, glad to have time alone with my thoughts. I dig through my closet.

Mom's not here, off to walk Leah home from school. She's been extra motherly since last weekend, when she hadn't come home and I had to take my sister to work.

But there will be no hiding that I'm going on this date. I share a room with my sister, so she'll notice when I start putting on makeup after dinner.

It's not like I haven't dated before. But none of those other short-lived relationships have felt anything like this.

Jason Packwood.

I locate the shoes. They're cheap but pristine, only worn once or twice. I lie back on the bed and imagine Jason's face in the water stains on the ceiling.

He's something.

But what do I know about him, really?

He's a friend of the Pickle family. Close enough that he considers their grandmother his own Grammy.

They're willing to go out on a limb for him. Even Jace Pickle's assistant. Although she did have some choice words about his bratty attitude.

Maybe it's time for some good old-fashioned cyber stalking.

I head to my desk and pull out my old laptop. It might have been invasive or weird to snoop while he was an unpaid intern forced on me by my boss.

But now, I think I have cause to look him up.

I power up the machine and type *Jason Packwood* into a search box.

It's a far more common name than I would've thought. There are vice presidents. A cardiologist. A real estate agent.

I scroll and scroll, but I don't see anybody that matches the Jason I know.

I finally spot a teen boy with similar features and click on the image.

It's from a small New York newspaper, talking about Jason Packwood's football legacy at the local high school.

I peer closer. I think it's him. His hair is longer and there's no facial scruff. But the eyes are just as bright, and he bears that same cocky smile.

This Jason Packwood was a senior twelve years ago. My Jason, according to his driver's license, is thirty.

The math adds up.

Now that I have a direct hit, I add the new details to see if I can narrow anything else down. I scroll through the potential Facebook matches. LinkedIn.

But there's nothing after 2008. Jason graduates high school and seems to disappear.

I click back on the football article and search the archives. Finally, I find a head and shoulders shot of Jason in his uniform. He was named player of the week.

"Who's that?" Leah asks. "He's cute!"

I plan to slam the laptop closed, but she's already spotted the resemblance. "Hey! That's Jason from Saturday."

"It is," I confess.

"Are you stalking him online?"

I turn to her. She looks like a ray of sunshine in a bright yellow Pokémon jacket.

"And what if I am?" I pull her close and tickle her belly, causing her to burst into giggles.

When she's escaped me to sit on the bed, she notices the clothes laid out. "Did you buy these?"

"They're Mom's. I'm borrowing them."

"Did you ask her? She might get mad."

I shrug. Mom isn't going to say anything about the clothes she bought with my college money.

"Are you going on a date with Jason?"

"Maybe."

She comes up behind me again. "Then I totally approve of you stalking him. He could be an axe murderer."

"What do you know about axe murderers?"

"I know they murder people with axes."

I yank her tight against me. "You don't need to worry about that. I've known Jason for a month and worked with him almost every day. He's not an axe murderer."

"I didn't think so. He likes my jokes!" She drops her elbows on my desk, chin in her hands. "What have you found?"

"Not much."

Leah peers at the screen. "He looks a lot different there."

"He's in high school. I can't find anything after he graduates."

"He probably realized social media was a waste of his time and energy."

"When did you get so wise?"

"They teach us about these things in fourth grade."

I power the computer down. "I guess I'll find out more about him tonight."

Leah returns to my bed. "Where y'all going?"

"Dinner, I think. We're meeting at the deli then deciding."

She sighs. "I wish I was going on a date with Jason."

I snatch her up from the bed, sending her into another burst of giggles. "Sisters don't take sister's dates!"

"You better treat him right!"

"He better treat *me* right!" My brain flashes to the epic orgasm on the mixing table. He does that, for sure. I aim Leah for the door. "You should get a snack. Tell Mom there's a new package of fruit bars in the pantry."

"My favorite!"

She takes off through the apartment.

I tuck the computer in my drawer. Maybe I'll get lucky, and we'll skip the awkward dinner and go straight to dessert.

When I pull up in front of Austin Pickle, Jason is already there.

I'm glad I chose the black skirt and silky shirt, because Jason is dressed like he's about to walk onto the set of a fashion show.

His black pants are creased so sharp they could cut butter. A white dress shirt, sleeves rolled up his forearm, have just the right number of buttons undone at the throat. A textured gray vest would put a groom to shame.

His ankles are crossed as he leans against the glass, watching me park. If someone snapped a picture of him, it would be worthy of a billboard.

And he is going out with *me*.

My entire belly quakes.

I'm not his boss right now. It's a date. He'll probably take me somewhere with six forks and three spoons. I won't know where to put my napkin or which glass to use.

It sure was a lot easier banging him in my office. Why did I agree to this?

He taps on my passenger window, his grin huge. I manage a weak smile and open my door. This part of downtown is quiet in the evenings. The office buildings are empty, and all the supporting restaurants and coffee shops close early, just like ours.

He strides around my car as I get out.

"Nova Strong, I didn't think you could get better than pink camo and a tank top, but I do believe you have knocked my socks off."

He bends down to brush a light kiss on my lips.

I don't have anything to say to that, but manage a quiet, "Thanks."

"I made a reservation for us," he says. "My chariot or yours?"

He gestures to a gleaming black BMW a couple of spots down from my beat-up Ford.

"I'd take mine," I say, "but I'm afraid the valet might put it out to pasture instead of parking it."

Jason laughs. "I love driving up to fancy places in unexpected cars," he says. "It tells me a lot about the business culture a company fosters among its employees."

"You really are always working angles, aren't you?"

"I think a lot about people and what makes someone friendly, or snobby, or rude." He holds out his hand. "But I am happy to drive if we're not up for experimenting today."

"Okay. Your car." I take his hand.

He opens the door for me, and from the moment I slide onto the smooth leather seats, my anxiety rises. I'm outclassed here. Completely. The only real question about how this evening will go is how I will thoroughly embarrass myself.

We cruise through the streets of downtown, past upscale condos where couples who look and dress like Jason emerge to walk their dogs along the sidewalk.

Funky boutiques with clever names show off their wares in glass windows, alternating with trendy restaurants focusing on a very specific type of food, like risotto or Korean barbecue or fish tacos. Many of them have outdoor seating bordered with iron fences, customers eating with their pets lying at their feet.

"It's too bad there isn't more sidewalk space in front of the deli for tables," Jason says.

"You might be able to squeeze a few narrow ones along the windows."

"Something to think about." He grins at me. "We're still talking about work."

"We are."

My nerves jangle so hard as we pull up into the circle drive of a hotel, I can hear them buzzing in my ears. The restaurant on the top floor is one of the fanciest places you can find in Austin.

Two young men approach the car, one coming around to open my door, and the other taking Jason's side.

"Welcome," mine says. He holds out his hand to help me out of the car.

No one's ever this courteous and subservient to me. I'm used to quick glances that swiftly dart away. Or your usual forced courtesy. The sort you do to avoid getting written up by your boss.

But I guess showing up in this car, this place, and maybe not wearing Army boots and camo, has made him act differently.

Jason meets me in front of the car and tucks my arm inside his. "I haven't been here since my last visit to Austin about a year ago. But the steaks are divine. No carnivore should miss it."

I nod, trying to quell my nerves. It's just a restaurant. I know about it, of course. A steak is almost a hundred dollars. A girl in my sociology class last year told me that. She was dating some older guy who took her here every weekend.

A doorman nods at us as we pass through the sliding glass door.

An older gentleman in a suit asks if we need any assistance. I bristle, thinking he's suggesting we don't belong.

"Just headed up top," Jason says easily.

"Very good, the elevators are to your left." He gives me a small bow. My belly still quakes. The feeling I don't belong here persists.

Jason presses a button on the elevator. After a moment, it slides open.

An older woman dressed in a form-fitted, all-white pantsuit steps out.

We shift aside to let her by.

She sees Jason first, appraising him admiringly from his shiny black dress shoes to his perfect scruff.

Then her gaze falls on me. Her face shifts into confusion, taking in my oversized shirt and knee-length skirt. The bargain bin dress pumps don't meet her approval.

Her lips pinch and her shoulders shift with a sharp twist as if she needs to turn away from the horrifying scene that is my outfit.

I glance over at Jason to see if he's noticed her disdain, but he's already heading toward the empty elevator, pulling on my hand.

No doubt when we get up top, there will be many more people like this lady. I don't want it. I don't live in one of the most casual big cities in the world only to end up at one of the few places where everyone will look down on me.

I plant my feet. "I don't think I'm up for this," I say.

He pulls back as the elevator doors close. "Is everything okay? You don't like it here?"

My whole body feels hot, like I'm burning from the inside out. "Maybe this is your lifestyle, but it's not mine."

Jason glances around, trying to figure out what might have prompted my outburst. "Okay, Nova. Let's blow this place off. I was trying to be, I don't know, a showoff." He runs his hand through his hair. "It's a thing with me. I overdo it. I should've known."

We hurry back toward the front door. I assume he's going to ask the valet to fetch his car, but he doesn't, taking us through the doors and across the grass to the street instead.

"Where are we going?" I wash over with chagrin, like I should've stuck it out. Is he mad? Why is he leaving his car?

"This is Austin," Jason says. "When in Austin, do like the Austinites."

He peels off his fancy vest, and the moment we pass a trash can, he tosses it in.

"Jason! Your clothes!"

"Don't need it. It was stupid anyway. Pretentious."

"Your car?"

"It can stay there."

We keep walking. "Where are we going now?"

"SoCo. You okay for a walk? Never mind. I'll get a pedicab."

When we arrive at the intersection, three pedicabs wait, their drivers perched on bicycles.

"Can you take us to SoCo?" Jason asks them.

"I will," a woman says. "Hop in."

We settle in the seat attached to the back of her bike, and she takes off down the street.

He puts his arm around me. "You up for some food trucks?"

My shoulders finally relax as we leave the towering hotel behind us. "I could totally go for some food trucks."

Despite it being the middle of the week, the food truck park is packed. We grab a pair of gyros from *Pitalicious* and walk along the sidewalk while we eat, looking in the shops.

Unlike the deli's part of downtown, South Congress is full of life. The doors to the costume shop *Lucy in Disguise* are thrown open, encouraging people to come in and look at their rooms full of costumes and vintage clothing.

We pass boutiques, gift shops, and tiny wine bars. Every place is crowded and full of energy.

As we approach the giant Mexican restaurant, *Gueros*, music spills out between the buildings.

"Aha," Jason says. "That's why it's so crazy down here. There's a concert tonight."

We drop our empty pita wrappers into a trash can, and Jason takes my hand again. "You want to see if we can get in?"

My head buzzes with the things I always worry about when trying to walk into busy places. Cover charges. Outrageous drink prices. But while I'm fretting, Jason waltzes straight up to a burly man in a taco T-shirt who sits on a stool inside the iron fence.

"Is it full?" he asks.

"There's room at the bar," he says. "Can I see your IDs?"

We flash him proof that we're old enough to drink and then, we're in.

A rollicking *Tejano* rock band plays on stage. The outdoor patio is packed, every bench and table full.

But the man was right. There are several open stools along the bar.

We head toward them and sit down. The bartender, madly filling pints of beer with both hands, gives us a quick nod of acknowledgment but keeps working.

This is a completely different culture than the fancy hotel, but still a good vibe that gives us confidence in their customer service. I don't know why I've never thought about this before.

I lean into Jason to say, "Why don't they teach us about business culture in class? Did you get that where you went to school?"

Jason doesn't answer for a moment, tapping his fingers to the beat on the scarred wood surface of the bar. "I think some things you need an instinct for. But once you see it, you'll always notice it."

The bartender heads our way, and we order a round of Shiners.

"At least you know what to drink in Austin," I say.

"That's one thing I miss when I'm up north. Shiner Bock. Austin Eastciders. But we have Tito's at least."

Our beers arrive, and I sip the Shiner. My belly is full of amazing pita. The air is cool but not cold. The beat of the music thumps through my body.

Jason scoots my stool closer to him and draws my back against his chest. He wraps his arms around me, and I let my head fall back onto his shoulder.

After everything that's happened this evening—his car, the valet, the woman on the elevator—this feels right. Like we finally found a place where we can coexist comfortably.

The air gets chillier, and we snuggle closer. Jason and I don't talk a lot, but we don't need to, letting the music wash over us. Just being here, out in the world, away from the deli, has been an experience that binds us.

The crowd starts to dwindle, and I shiver against him.

"My condo is only four blocks from here," he whispers in my ear. "You want to come?"

At last.

I turn on my stool to wrap my hands around his neck. "I think the real question is: How many times?"

23

JACE

I don't even show her around my place. The evening has been torture, her body against mine at the bar, my arms around her.

The minute my front door closes, I'm on her, kissing her hair, unbuttoning that silky blouse. I want her naked, to worship her. I want her in every corner of this apartment, again and again, until I'm annihilated.

We fall onto my sofa, a tangle of arms and legs. I kiss everything I can get to, her lips, her neck, the swell of her breasts.

"I could live on the feast of your body," I say, pushing her skirt up to her waist to reveal those soft thighs and the "V" of her black panties. God, I'm wild for those.

I have to hold myself back from tearing off everything. I want her. I'm insatiable, driven mad for her. I know we have a conversation ahead about who I am, but I can't do it now. Not yet. I need her. I'm a dying man, and she is my last wish.

She pulls at the buttons of my shirt, wrestling it over my shoulders. I toss it and make quick work of hers, sending it fluttering across the room.

"You are so damn beautiful," I tell her. "I want to plaster my walls with life-size images of every inch of you."

I'm careless with the panties and tear straight through the lace. I can't even apologize, dragging her legs wide so I can dive into her, lapping with my tongue. This is where I've wanted to be. Pleasuring her, making her cry out. She can't let me go if I'm here, loving her in this exquisite place we find together.

Her hips rock up to me, and I lift her ass to give me deeper access. My gaze roves up her body, bisected by the bunched-up skirt, her belly writhing, her bra barely containing those breasts.

I reach up and release one from the black lacy cup. The nipple responds to my touch, tight and budded beneath my thumb. She crosses one arm over her face, her lips parted.

I never want this moment to end.

I take it easy, controlling her, bringing her to that peak and holding her there. She grips the sofa cushion, crushing herself into my face.

My mouth keeps its steady, rocking pressure. She's so wet, so eager.

"Jason," she says. "Please. God."

I can't resist anything she asks, and dive in, circling the nub, licking end to end with long, luscious pressure.

She comes hard, jolting upwards, her cry almost a

scream. "Jason, Jason, Jason." Her muscles spasm every time she says my name.

I slow my movements, bringing her down. I almost shake inside. Fuck. I don't want this to end. I can't let her go. Fear sluices through me. When this is over, when she finds out, will she leave me right away?

I don't realize I've pressed my cheek to her belly until she curves around me. "Hey, you okay?" Her fingers trail across my head. "We're all right. It's fine that you took me to that fancy place. I'll try harder next time to fit in. I can't expect you to give up your whole world for me."

She has no idea. I already have. I don't want anything else but her.

It's time to tell her. Fess up.

I lift my head. Her expression is nothing like what I've seen on Nova before. Tender. Concerned. She cares.

But I know her. She's fire and anger and strength. My words will cut through this gentleness she's feeling.

"It's not that," I say.

"Good," she interrupts. "Because it's time you take me to your bed and fuck me properly."

She shifts away from me and stands. "I think maybe you need a little inspiration."

Her skirt slides back into place. She's a goddess in a black bra. The confession dies on my tongue.

She turns away and looks at me over her shoulder. "Where's your phone?"

I pull it out. "What do you want to do with it?"

"I want you to use it."

I swallow. "What for?"

"Shut off your upload to the cloud."

"I don't use that."

"Good."

She bends over, and the sweet pink of her recently worked parts peek out from under the skirt. "Take a picture. You said you wanted to plaster your walls with me."

Fuuuuuck. I lift my phone and take the shot.

She stands and reaches behind her to unhook the bra. "No faces."

"Wouldn't dare."

She slowly slides it down her arms, still facing away. "Ready?"

"Born ready." All other thoughts in my head are blown out.

She tosses the bra and lifts her arms in the air. She turns slightly, until one perfect breast, topped with a pert pink nipple comes into view. "Got it?"

I snap, like, five hundred shots.

This is so hot I think I'm going to explode.

She comes closer. "Now give the phone to me."

I almost hesitate. The phone could be my undoing if she gets even a glimpse of my contacts. But I give it over.

She straddles me, pressing her perfect round breasts into my face. "Look up."

I do.

She takes the shot, my face buried in her glorious naked chest. She turns it for me to see.

Fuuuuuck.

"Jason's personal porn." She tosses the phone on the sofa. "Now, take me the hell to bed."

I don't make her ask twice.

24

___

NOVA

I know I made a big show of nonchalance out there, but as Jason takes my hand to lead me to his bedroom, I'm quaking in my bargain bin heels. And skirt. And nothing else.

Jason's condo is sleek and modern and perfectly furnished. The only way you even know someone lives here are the scattered coins on the dresser and several shirts thrown over a chair in the corner. One of them is the Pickle shirt I gave him after we cleaned the bathrooms.

He must have a housekeeper or something. I've never seen a single man's place look like this.

His bed isn't made, though, so nobody's been there today. It helps me, seeing the navy comforter in disarray, the pillow askew. As if Jason's not all the way perfect. He's human like the rest of us.

He sits on the end of the bed and pulls me close. I'm taller in the heels, and his hair tickles the underside of my breasts. He wraps his arms around my hips and holds me tightly.

I run my fingers through his hair, wondering how he's doing. It's been an up-and-down night, that's for sure. Finally, I kick off the shoes and inch up the skirt so I can sit on his lap. This brings our faces closer together.

"You okay?" I ask. His emotions have turned. It's an entirely different Jason than I've seen before, quiet and introspective.

He nods, and his hands lift to hold each side of my face. His gaze meets mine, eyes glittery in the bit of light coming from a table lamp near the door.

"Good, because I have no idea how to get to your car or mine. I'm at your mercy." My grin teases a small smile from him.

"I think I like Nova Strong at my mercy."

He rolls us over, neatly shifting us up the bed to fall in the middle. The flannel sheets are soft and warm. "I could get all cozy in these," I say, dragging one over me.

"Oh no, you don't," he says, pulling the sheet away. "And away with this." He finds the zipper on the skirt and slides it down.

We've had four encounters so far, and he's never put his own pleasure before mine. As he tosses my skirt away from the bed, I shift to my knees. "I believe I'm in charge here," I tell him.

"Is that a direct order from my superior?"

"It might be."

Jason falls back on the white sheets, his hands clasped behind his head. He's like a Greek god sitting there, shirtless, every muscle in his chest and abs on display.

"Am I getting a performance review?" he asks.

We're back to our light banter, and this is easier than the serious version of him.

"There seems to be some pickle mismanagement going on." I unbuckle his leather belt and sinuously slide it from the loops.

"Is there? How can I correct it?"

I unfasten the button of his fly. "I'll need to take inventory to know."

He swallows hard as I lower the zipper and spread apart his fly. Below it, he wears black fitted boxers.

"It seems the goods are all stacked to one side."

"Should we rotate the stock?"

"Good idea."

I grasp the elastic band and pull it down. Jason Packwood's impressive erection lifts away from his belly.

"I feel like we need a clever new name for this new pickle offering," I say.

He laughs. "Like the pickle of the month?"

"Exactly."

"Big Pickle?"

"Maybe." I run my thumb along the head. "Head salami?"

"Except I'm only a lowly vegetable slicer."

"Thoughts?"

"Mayo cannon?"

My hand stills. "Jason! Gross!"

He grasps my waist, tossing me back onto the sheets. Before I can react, he's got me on my back, and I'm pinned, his legs straddling me this time, the *mayo cannon* aimed right at me.

He leans down and kisses me, his hard chest brushing against mine. I feel light and happy.

His hair tickles my belly, and I draw my knees up on either side of him. "A bed," I say. "How ordinary."

His teeth flash in the dark as he grins up at me. "I know."

He kicks off his shoes and shucks the pants. I ease the boxers down his thighs until we're in a place that's new, fully naked, skin-to-skin, comfortable and warm.

His hands learn every curve and valley of me, and I explore the rugged terrain of his muscles, belly, and thighs. We take our time, looking, kissing, touching, memorizing textures and those unexpected spots that elicit a sharp intake of breath.

When he finally slides into my body this time, it's a connection, a perfect fit. I clutch his back, his face tucked against my ear. He moves slowly, sinuously, like a spool of ribbon unfurling.

I'm moved, emotionally caught, the pleasure in it not purely from the muscles and the friction, but the chorus of our bodies, two melodies that intertwine.

There's no rapid-fire plunging, no gasping. Just a gentle pressure that gradually increases in intensity, like a sunrise, like dawn.

We hold each other, reveling in each incremental rise, until the rhythm takes a life of its own. My body clenches around him, pulsing, drawing life from him into me with an orgasm that is effortless, smooth, and deep. He responds, spilling out, breathing harder, his arms so tight around me that I'm not sure where I end and he begins.

We come down into a relaxation that melts us to the bed. My hair is everywhere. Our bodies are sprawled in every direction.

But I feel such peace.

I don't have to be in charge here. Not like at the deli. Or with my mom and sister. I'm not responsible for anyone or anything in this moment.

I'm just a woman, in bed with an incredible man. As he softly kisses my head through my hair, I realize this is more than a bang in the backroom of my workplace.

I have something very real, and very perfect.

25

JACE

I wake in my condo with a start. Something's off.

I roll over to Nova.

She's not there.

The bed is cold.

I look at the clock.

Almost seven? It's time to make the bread!

I jump up, glancing around. Damn! I hurry to the bathroom. Empty.

When I flip on the light in the living room, I spot a sheet of paper. I pick it up.

Jason—I've had enough. I never want to see you again.

What?

My stomach hollows out, then I realize there's a second page.

. . .

April Fools!
    My favorite holiday.

Oh, I'm going to get her good for that.
    There's more.

Didn't want to wake you. Lamonte will help me with the bread. No rush!

I set the pages down.
    But my heart won't stop hammering.
    She's gone.
    I didn't confess.
    All those chances last night.
    But the evening…it was so…
    Images flash through my memory. Nova sprawled on my sofa. Taking off her bra. Photographs. Sighs. That pure perfection in my bed. The contentedness. The rightness.
    There has to be a way to confess what I've done without killing all that. My being Jace Pickle should change nothing.
    Except trust.
    The trust she has felt in no one, not even her own mother. The trust she lost, realizing someone was taking money from the safe at the deli.
    The trust she placed in me, as part of her team, a

trust that expanded to her bed, her passion, her vulnerability.

And I've broken it.

I have to make this right.

When I arrive at the deli half an hour later, an unfamiliar middle-aged man stands in front of the open cabinet that houses the safe.

My whole body goes on alert. "Who the hell are you?" I demand.

Lamonte emerges from Bertha carrying two sacks of flour. "Stand down, big man, this is the locksmith to fix the safe. Apparently, the dial's busted."

He drops the bags on the mixing table and heads back to the pantry.

Right. Nova said she hired someone to show her how to recalibrate the combination when we were ready to lock out the thief, if we ever caught him. Interesting that she didn't tell Lamonte the real reason why.

I walk over to her office door, which is open only a crack.

She's on the phone. When she sees me, she waves me inside and motions for me to close the door.

"Look, I said I had a narrow window for you to install this thing. If you can't be here by eight o'clock, I don't want you here at all."

She gives me a look of abject frustration.

"Then you have to come after we close. The whole

point is to put the cameras in so no one on staff knows they're there."

She goes quiet again.

"Okay. Four o'clock is fine. I'll ask my cleaning crew to wait until you're done to come in. Don't be late. OR early."

She drops her phone on the desk.

"Should I go rough someone up for you?" I ask and gather her into my arms. She feels so amazing there. Her hair is damp and smells of my shampoo. How did I sleep through her shower and everything? The thought of Nova naked in my bath gives me a new life goal.

"I'm trying not to let anyone in on the fact that we're about to start spying."

"Lamonte seems to think the safe is broken."

She buries her face in my chest. "He's one of my best friends. But I don't want to assume anything. I want to do this right."

I slide my hand down her back, reveling in the feel of her. "I'm sure it's not Lamonte."

She pulls away and paces the tiny office. "Then who could it be? Kate? Eli? Arush? Connie or Charlotte? I know all these people so well. How could they steal from this deli?"

"We don't know that it's our own staff."

"But Jace Pickle owns this building," Nova argues. "It's not like there are outside people who come in when we're not here."

She has a point, and I can see this problem has weighed on her since we figured out cash had gone missing.

"We'll catch them," I say.

"I hate knowing for a fact someone is stealing and letting them keep doing it. I want to change the combination. Make it stop."

"But then we can't catch them."

"What do we do then? Call the police?"

"Probably," he says. "You have to file a report. This has to be dealt with."

She drops into her chair. "I don't feel qualified for this."

I kneel in front of her and take her hand. "I don't think anyone ever does."

There are three short raps on the door, then Lamonte barges in. When he sees me kneeling in front of Nova, her hand in mine, he stops short. "I knew it. I told Kate there was something going on." He crosses his arms over his chest. "Actually, she told me. I was blind as a bat. But we were right. You two have become a thing."

Nova pushes out a great gust of air. "We'd appreciate it if you kept this quiet. It's not been going on for long. Just a couple of days."

"Whatever you say, Miss Sparkle Eyes. But the locksmith needs you for something."

"I'm coming."

Lamonte heads out. I'm about to walk out the door when Nova calls me back. "Jason?"

I turn around the doorway. "Yeah?"

"I did have fun last night. It was..." She trails off and our eyes lock for a long moment.

"I know exactly what you're trying to say," I tell her. "And I agree."

We share a small smile. I think my confession will have to wait. For one, it's April Fool's Day. Nobody tells anyone anything important on a day like this.

Two, we need to catch a thief. I have to finish what I came here to do. Let work life settle down again for Nova. She's got too much to bear right now.

As I survey the mixing table, and how far Lamonte has gotten on the bread, I head to Mr. Chill to pick up the next set of ingredients he'll need.

And consider how much time I have left with Nova before I tell her the truth.

26

NOVA

The stupid security man is late again.

I help Connie and Charlotte clean the deli, trying to push them through before he gets here.

I don't suspect either of them in the stealing, I really don't. But like I told Jason, I want to do this right. Assume nothing.

Connie gives Jason a broom, and the two of us sweep.

When he gets close to me, he asks, "When's the guy coming?"

"Hell if I know. I'm about to fire him."

He grins. "I'd like to see that."

There's a different feel to our conversations today. I know it's about last night. I did sneak away, taking the fastest shower possible and using my phone to navigate the downtown streets until I made it to the deli.

It was a bit of a walk, a couple of miles, but it was good to clear my head.

Things have gotten intense so fast. I feel like I don't

know anything about him. His family. What he plans to do after his time in Austin. I'm privy to very little of his history, other than the fact he played football in high school.

Which I can't bring up without admitting I stalked him.

What are we even doing?

As he holds a dustpan for me to sweep the crumbs from the deli floor, his smile is so genuine, and his gaze is so earnest, I don't think I can suspect him of anything terrible.

If he's playing some game with me, I can't see it. And even if I'm a short-term fling, it's not as if I didn't know he was temporary.

Although he does have a really nice condo for someone only visiting. Maybe it's a short-term rental. That would explain the cleanliness.

Charlotte follows behind us, swiftly mopping the floor. We'll easily be done in half the usual time, but I'm mindful of the hours they need.

As we finish up, I tell them, "Go ahead and write down the usual hours. We need to be able to shut down earlier tonight."

The women ask no questions, happy for less work and an early night. When they finally close the back door, Jason asks, "So I guess we wait here for this guy?"

My annoyance simmers beneath the surface, threatening to boil into anger. "If he's not here in the next half hour, I say we lock up and he's fired. I can find someone else."

But the words are no more out of my mouth when a

tap on the front glass draws us back into the front. It's the security guy. He's mid-thirties, with a mega-beard and a beer gut.

As I unlock the door, I am ready to lay into him.

But he speaks first. "Thank you so much for understanding today," he says. "My wife is due any day now, and twice she's called me home thinking she's in labor. I'll get these cameras installed lickety-split; in case I get another one."

"Oh!" I say. "Are you sure you should be here?"

The man waves me off. "This shouldn't take an hour. You want everything remote and wireless, right? It's running wire that takes forever."

"Yes, wireless," I say.

He wanders through the deli. "I assume you want something over the register, and front door? You asked for a five-camera system."

I follow the man. "Yes. Front door. Back door. Cash register. Office. Safe."

"Show me the other spots. Then I'll get all the gear from my truck."

I give the man a rundown of what I'd like, and Jason and I take down a couple of chairs from a table to sit and wait.

"Thanks for hanging out with me," I say. "You don't have to if you have something else to do."

Jason leans in close. "The only thing I want to do right now is *you*."

"We've been pretty insatiable, haven't we?" It's new to me, this every day, twice a day, can't-stop-thinking-about-it one-track mind.

He waggles his eyebrows at me. "And now we can do it on camera."

"What! No!" But he's right. The camera in my office will keep us from going in there.

We didn't think this through.

Within half an hour, the man tells us he's installed the cameras, and we need to load the software on my computer to activate them.

The three of us head into my office, and the security guy shows us the varying views of the cameras and the settings to store the recordings.

"You might want to get an external hard drive for this," he says. "They take up a lot of room."

"This is great. Thank you."

He scribbles some numbers on his clipboard and passes me the sheet. "Here's the invoice. You can mail it in."

I set the paper down. "Thank you. And good luck with the baby. Is it your first?"

He shoves the clipboard in his rolling cart. "Number six," he says.

"Well," Jason says. "That's something."

"Tell me about it." He rolls his cart through the kitchen. "I can see myself out. Thank you for your patience today."

"No problem!" I call.

I return to the screen, watching the image of the man pass under the register camera and then fall out of view again, picking back up on the camera to the front door.

"This is pretty good," I say.

Jason picks up my keys. "I'll go lock the front door."

I turn to him. "And then what?"

His grin is full of mischief. "We get started on our own six kids."

My jaw drops, but he laughs and heads out across the kitchen.

I watched him follow the same path as the security guy, admiring his confident stride.

And his butt in those jeans.

I know I should ask him what we're doing, where we're going, what his plans are. But this time together has been so full of magic, I don't want to question it. Just live in the moment. Enjoy what I have while it lasts.

When I hear the swinging door, I call out, "Hey, go walk near the safe and by the back door so I can follow your movements and see how they look in here."

"Sure."

He appears by the safe cabinet first, looking up and waving.

When he arrives at the back door, his face peers up into the camera. "So, who's going to review this footage?"

"Just me, I guess," I call.

He grasps the bottom of his shirt and pulls it off.

"Jason!"

"You said it was just you!"

"For now!"

He starts unbuckling his belt.

"Hey! I might have to turn it over to the police!"

Jason hesitates. "I guess I shouldn't give some random cop a show."

I head to the door of my office. "I don't think so."

He walks slowly toward the office. "What about here?"

I turned to look at the screen on my desk. "I can still see you."

He takes a few more steps forward. "Here?"

"That seems to be a dead spot."

He holds out his arms. "All of this?"

I shake my head. "I can see your fingertips."

He comes to the door. "The camera gets your entire office."

"Yep."

"Can we turn off a single camera?"

"Probably. But I would have to figure out how."

He frowns. "Well, I guess that's it. Our sex lives are over."

I shove at his chest. "Am I not as interesting in your bed as I am in the office?"

"Oh, I like you both places. But asking me to wait an entire workday might be too much."

I lean back against the door frame. "So, what are you going to do about it?"

He glances around the kitchen. "Did we get a delivery of flour today?"

"We did."

"So, there's lots of big cloth bags in the pantry?"

I don't know where he's going with this. "I guess so. I haven't been there."

"Good enough for me." He picks me up and throws me over his shoulder.

The world tilts as I'm turned upside down. I

pummel his backside as he holds onto my legs. "Hey. Caveman! What are you doing?"

"Me find dark cave. Me take woman to cave with no security cameras."

He carries me the short distance to the door of Bertha and reaches up to flip on the light.

"In here?" I ask.

"In here." He sets me down on a pile of flour sacks and turns to look out into the kitchen. "Goodbye cameras!" he says and shuts the door.

He grabs the hem of my shirt and whips it over my head.

I realize when it comes to Jason and his interest in me, if there is a will, there's a way.

27

JACE

April starts out pretty sweet.

Nova and I stay late every day, checking the cash in the safe and reviewing the footage from the cameras from the previous night.

But for two weeks, nothing happens. It's if they somehow know we're on to them.

I don't care. I can't get enough of Nova. She's always willing and eager. Sometimes we're playful in our roles as lowly intern and boss.

Sometimes it gets more serious, and we lie together for hours, talking about inconsequential things.

Sometimes she stays over. Sometimes she goes home to spend time with her sister. We've made an unspoken rule about staying apart on Sundays when the deli is closed. Since we work together all week, it makes sense to find time for other things.

Today's a Monday, and with the cameras every-where, we've had to be good all day.

Nova sits back in her chair, Army boots up on the

desk, ankles crossed. I run my finger along the bit of skin between her rolled-up pant leg and the sock peeking out over the top of the boot. Touching her skin anywhere sets off a hum in my body.

Our eyes meet, and I know she's thinking what I'm thinking—time to go.

"Should I check the safe?" she asks. "We don't have to stay while the girls finish cleaning. They have a key."

I continue the slow easy caress on her leg. "Sure. If there isn't any money missing, there's no point checking the footage."

So far, there hasn't been a point in any of it. I'm surprised. If whoever was pilfering cash was going to unexpectedly stop, they would have quit when Susan left. And if not then, at least when Nova got the keys and took over.

But it went on, in sporadic amounts, every few days.

Right until we installed the cameras.

I don't get it. We've been careful not to make any mention of the missing money to anyone. No one should know we're watching. We've kept the cash routine exactly the same.

Nova sets her boots on the floor. "I'll go take a peek. I'm sure it's the same story as every day."

While she's gone, I flip through the camera views. I keep my eye on the office door, to make sure neither Connie nor Charlotte sees the feed.

The cameras are super subtle. Very small, the ceiling tiles cut to fit them so only the barest hint of the glass shows.

But it's possible whoever was watching to see when

the deli was empty happened to notice the security truck out front. Or maybe they watched for cameras to be installed, particularly after Nova took over.

So, they've moved on.

I wonder how long I should wait before calling this problem over. And after that, how much longer I should stay.

I don't want to go. In fact, if things don't go completely south when I tell Nova who I am, maybe I'll take up residence in Austin. I honestly don't mind the hours or the work. We have a good crew and it's fun.

And with Kate leaving in a month, I should probably oversee the other people we hire. Maybe even hire an assistant manager and give Nova some time off. As it stands, she can't easily take a vacation. The deli could run a day or two without her, but beyond that, someone would need to step in.

If I'm with her, hopefully watching her sunbathe topless on the Riviera, I won't be able to help out either.

Just the thought of that vacation dream sends me over the edge. I'm ready to get out of here. I adjust my jeans and stand up to see what's taking Nova so long.

But suddenly, she bursts into the office and closes the door behind her.

"Money's missing," she says quickly. "Exactly five hundred dollars. Like the old days. That's no coincidence. Something's happened."

She's shaking. I take the packet of cash from her and set it on the desk. "You okay?"

"I don't know. I mean we knew it was happening. But for it to happen while we're watching. It's a lot. So I guess it was last night? Some thief?" She wraps her arms around her body like she's cold.

I sit in her desk chair and draw her onto my lap. "Let's look at the footage together. I think this is about to be over. We'll see who it is."

She nods, her hand gripping my thigh.

"I'm so afraid," she whispers. "Please don't be anyone we care about."

I click the settings to find the recordings that began at close of yesterday. "That's why we're looking at it ourselves first. Then we can make some decisions."

"We have to tell Jace Pickle either way," she says. I try not to flinch at my name. "He may not care if it's someone we love who might be desperate for reasons we don't know."

My jaw tightens. "Let's cross that bridge only if we come to it. I really don't think we will."

But as we pull up the safe footage and begin quickly scrubbing through the recording, I wonder if I can stop what will happen. This is not a small amount of money. At the height of the theft, it was a couple thousand a week for months on end.

There are issues of insurance, and the franchise itself. What would my dad want me to do?

Nova lunges forward. "Stop."

I scrub backward. A figure appears in the corner of the frame. She turns, and it's clearly a woman. She doesn't glance around but reaches up to make sure her hood covers her head.

"What does the back of her hoodie say?" Nova asks.

I pause the video, but that makes it even harder to

read. The resolution isn't high enough for a still. I reverse a few frames and start it again.

"Something cleaning service," I say.

"We don't use a cleaning service. Connie and Charlotte are employees of the deli. Not a service."

"What about that time they were sick?"

"I hired Connie's sister. Still not a service."

We fall quiet as we watch the woman bend down, presumably to open the safe and combination lock.

"Is that the sister?"

"No. She was much larger."

The woman blocks the view of the camera. We can't see her actions, and it wouldn't be enough for law enforcement. "We can't even see her face," I say.

The woman stands, closes the cabinet again, and walks out of the frame.

Nova braces her elbows on the desk. "We proved it's somebody. Which we already knew."

"I think we also know it's nobody who works for us. This clearly is not Connie, Charlotte, Kate, or Elda. You ruled out Connie's sister."

"But we don't know anything about this woman. Her hair color or anything." Nova frowns at the screen as I play through the woman's actions at the safe a second time.

"I guess we have to catch her in the act."

"Are you crazy? What if she has a gun? Or some thugs waiting out in the car as backup if she gets in trouble?"

I slide her mouse closer. "Let's look at the backdoor footage. Maybe there's a better view."

"Good idea," Nova says. "I'm glad you're here. I'm freaking out so hard I can't think."

I switch views and forward to a few minutes before the safe footage began.

"There she is," Nova says.

The woman enters the back door of the deli holding a broom.

"She's making it look like she's legitimately here," I say. "She's banking on the fact nobody will be concerned with her appearance at the back door."

Nova nods. "She has to look legit. I'm sure that's probably a fake cleaning service."

"Probably."

The woman sets the broom against the wall and carefully closes the door. "This is dark," Nova says. "There's a light on by the time she gets to the safe."

With the door closed, the woman is a shadowy figure, but her hand reaches out for the light. She fumbles for a while, running her hand along the wall, and eventually flips it on.

"She didn't know where the switch was," Nova says.

"She doesn't work here, then, and never has."

Nova nods in agreement.

The door camera only catches the side and back of the woman as she walks out of range toward the safe.

"Maybe when she comes back, we'll get a glimpse of her face," I say.

We scrub forward until she enters the range of the door camera again. She keeps her head down, picks up her broom, flips off the light, and quietly exits through the back.

I stop the footage. "We can't identify her from this. I guess we have to move on to phase two."

Nova leans back against my chest. "What's that?"

"We set up an alarm so we can catch her in the act."

"How can we get here fast enough? You want to hide here in the office?"

"Maybe." I wrap my arms tightly around her waist. "If we turn the lights off in here, the camera can't pick up what we're doing while we wait."

She laughs lightly, and I feel her relax a bit.

"It won't hurt to install an alarm," Nova says. "But I don't like the idea of us confronting her. There are crazy, desperate people in the world. Besides, we can stop her. We just have to change the combination lock and she can't steal anymore."

I rest my chin on her shoulder. "I know we could stop her. But I'd like to figure out how the hell she has the key and combination. If the ex-manager is involved, she shouldn't get away with this."

"There is that."

"I can pick up a simple alarm at the hardware store that will send a notification to my phone. Maybe we can mark some of the bills. If she has them on her when we call the police over the alarm, that will be serious evidence against her even if the video doesn't pick up her face."

Nova turns to me. "You're full of good ideas."

"I was sent here to solve the case. We're a regular Sherlock and Holmes."

Nova shifts in my lap and wraps her arms around

my neck. "You have to be Holmes, because I look good in plaid."

"You look good in everything."

"You look good in nothing."

"Let's get out of here and make sure."

So, we do.

28

NOVA

After the lunch rush is over the next day, Jason heads to the store to pick up a door alarm.

Despite everything happening with our mystery, I walk through the deli with a sense of confidence I haven't felt since we learned someone was stealing. None of my people are involved, and I'm completely relieved. Hopefully, within a day or two this whole thing will be over.

Jason returns shortly after the bulk of the crew has left. I sit in my office with a Sharpie, adding my initials to the top corner of random bills to sprinkle throughout the stack of cash.

Lamonte pokes his head into my office while I work. "Defacing money? Isn't that a felony?" He plunks down in the chair next to me.

"Just trying to leave my mark on the world," I say. "And I looked it up. It's only illegal if you destroy the currency. Besides, everyone's putting Harriet Tubman on the twenties."

"True. So, where did Jason take off to?"

"He had some errand to run today."

Lamonte shifts in the chair, then bends to straighten the roll of his jean cuff. He's been growing out some baby dreads, and I reach out to tweak one. "I love these."

He runs his hand over them. "They take forever."

"I bet." I sense he has something to say to me, but he's beating around the bush. "So, what's up?"

"I don't want to get weird because you're my friend, not just the boss, but…"

I set down the Sharpie to give him my full attention, my heart racing. Is he involved in the theft after all? Does he know we saw the woman? Is she a friend?

I work hard to keep the waver out of my voice. "What's going on?"

His eyes turn down to the floor. "I'm gonna need more hours, or a raise or something, or I'll have to find another place to work. I can't hold things together where I'm at."

My pulse slows to a normal pace. It's a simple employee matter. "Maybe we can work something out. How long have you been here? Six months?"

"Five and change."

I swivel in my chair. "Can you move up to full-time?"

"I always could. There was never room for more full-timers."

"That's because I didn't know our budget or what I could do. I've been thinking about adding an assistant manager. We used to have one. Let me see if I can get in touch with Jace Pickle about it."

"Really? You'd make me assistant manager?"

"You've been here as long as anyone except Elda, and she always says she doesn't want any job other than the one she's got."

"So I'd get more hours and a raise?"

"As long as I can convince the owner."

He practically bounces in the chair. "That's great! Dang! Dang!"

"I'll try to call him in the morning." I pick up the Sharpie again.

He stands but then pauses at the door. "I noticed Jason's been making the bread every morning. What are you gonna do when he's gone?"

His words are like a rock settling in my gut. "I guess I'll figure that out when it happens."

"Don't you let him break your heart." He crosses his arms over the chest of his Austin City Limits T-shirt. "I won't put up with that. Not with my girl."

"It was always going to be a temporary thing," I say. "I can handle it."

"I've seen you two."

I wave him away. "I'll let you know what Jace Pickle says."

Lamonte takes off, and I listen for the opening and closing of the back door. I'm alone in the deli, waiting for either Jason to come back or Connie and Charlotte to show up to clean. I mark a few more bills and pile them together, carefully placing them in the same locking bag I've used all this time.

I hold the heavy canvas bag in my hands. The zipper has a three-digit spinner you have to roll to the right combination to open it.

Whoever's been stealing knows everything. Safe. Zipper combo. She obviously isn't part of my current crew, but was she part of the old one?

As I take the money to the safe to possibly be stolen by this mystery woman, I run through all the people I knew when I first worked there. Do we have a list somewhere? We should have applications and other documents that would refresh my memory about who worked here when I first started.

I double check that the front door is locked and the *Closed* sign out. When I return to the kitchen, Jason comes in through the back door.

"I was beginning to think you'd gotten lost."

"This was harder to find than I thought."

"Let me have the receipt, and I'll make sure you're reimbursed."

He waves me away. "We can worry about that later." He drops the box on the mixing table. "I mainly want to get this thing installed."

I glance at the clock. "Connie and Charlotte will be here any minute. Do you care if they see since it's not them?"

He picks the box back up. "We don't know who knows this woman. She could get tipped off, even accidentally if someone who works here doesn't realize what they're doing. We'll open it up in your office. Then we can install it before we leave."

By the time Connie and Charlotte are done with

their tasks, Jason has laid out all the pieces of the alarm, along with the tools he'll need. It's a simple set up, a beam that breaks when the door opens.

When Jason has screwed it all in, we test it by opening the door. His phone immediately buzzes with an alert.

"Perfect," he says. "Now we wait."

"We're not waiting here, are we?" My heart hammers. I'm still afraid she'll have a weapon on her for protection. Jace Pickle's money is not something to get killed over.

"I'm willing to bet she'll come the same time as last night. I think we should go about our merry way this evening and around ten fifteen, park across the street and see if the alarm goes off."

"It might be two weeks before she returns."

"It might." He pulls me close. "I'm happy to make out with you in the car while we wait."

We park a block down from the deli a little after ten. We don't want to be too close, in case the person drives up the street and is spooked by a car nearby.

"So, what exactly is our plan?" I ask.

Jason's face is lit by his phone screen as he answers. "Alarm goes off. I call the police, and we drive around the corner to see where she goes when she leaves the building."

"If we follow her, who's going to be there when the police arrive?"

Jason frowns. "We'll have to let her go."

I clasp my hands tightly in my lap. "Don't you think we should have called the police already?"

"Until yesterday, we thought this was an inside job. That's a company matter."

"It's still an inside job. The person has the combination to the safe."

"I guess if she doesn't come tonight, we'll let the Pickles know what we've found."

"You think Jace Pickle will be upset we didn't tell him right away?"

"I think he'll appreciate our efforts to figure it out."

We sit in silence for a moment. Jason seems so sure he understands what Jace Pickle would want.

I'm about to ask him if he's talked directly to Jace about the theft, when his entire phone jingles with noise. The door alert comes up on screen.

"That's it," he says. "The alarm has been tripped."

He eases the car forward as he dials 911.

I lean over to look through the glass. The streetlights create a reflection. I can only see the barest shadows inside.

But then, the circle of the window in the swinging door brightens. "She flipped on the light!"

Jason's call clicks through. I hear the muted woman's voice. "911, what is your emergency?"

"Robbery in progress," Jason says quickly. He gives the address of the deli. "They're in there right now. They tripped my alarm."

"I'll send someone right away. Are you in any danger?"

"No. We're in our car across the street. We suspected someone was stealing and set up an alarm to catch them."

"Just stay on the line, sir," the woman says. "The police are on the way."

Jason turns to me. "Should we drive around?" he mouths.

My belly is shaking. I press my arms against it. "I guess it won't hurt to turn the corner."

He nods and hits the gas.

Every sound seems amplified. The hum of the engine. The woman's voice, telling him not to intervene. The swish of tires on the asphalt.

"Don't go in the alley," I say.

He stops at the intersection where the alley dumps onto the street.

We peer at the building. The back door of the deli is not completely closed, and a small sliver of light escapes into the dark.

"There's no car anywhere," I say.

Jason nods. The woman on the line asks for Jason's name and phone number and he gives it. But something in his words catches my attention. I don't remember those being the last four digits of his number.

I pull out my phone and scroll through my contacts.

No. Those definitely are not his last four digits.

I'm about to tell him he gave the wrong phone number to the woman when the light in the alley clicks out.

"She's about to take off," he says into the phone.

But even as he says it, bright flashing lights in red

and blue hurtle toward us. As the police car approaches, Jason yanks open his door and jumps out in the street.

"That way! That way!" He sends the squad car into the alley.

The officer rolls in that direction.

The woman's shape lights up in the swirl of color. She takes off running.

I shove open my door as a second police car arrives from the other direction. I'm not sure what to do.

Jason runs down the alley, slightly behind the first police car.

My breath rushes fast as I clutch the roof of the car. I feel like I'm going to pass out.

A tinny woman's voice gets my attention. I duck my head back in the car. Jason has left his phone on his seat. I pick it up.

"We're okay," I say to the woman. "The police are here." I end the call and shove Jason's phone in my jeans pocket.

The police cars have raced down the alley, but a third one arrives at the far end.

The woman is trapped. Jason hangs out near the back door of the deli, well away from the woman or the cops. I press my hand to my heart, thankful he's out of range of whatever might happen.

I head across the street. The police cars stop on either side of the woman. She drops to her knees.

One of the officers jumps out. "Hands up!" he orders the woman.

The woman lifts her arms in the air, and I let out a long breath.

They got her.

By the time we walk up, the woman is already handcuffed.

"Are you the one who called this in?" the officer asks. "Stay back."

"We did," Jason says.

"Who's the owner?" The man's face lights up red and blue from the lights.

"His name is Jace Pickle," I say. "I'm the manager." I avoid looking at the woman on the ground, surrounded by two other officers.

The man nods and jots something in a notebook.

"Will you take her in?" Jason asks. While he talks to the officer, I pull out my phone and find Jace's number in my contacts. He needs to know what's happened.

I initiate the call, and immediately, my pocket buzzes.

It's Jason's cell.

Jason turns to me right as I pull out his phone.

And there it is, right in front of me. My name on the caller ID.

On Jason's phone.

Which is apparently Jace Pickle's phone.

The ground falls away from my feet. I can't find my bearings, and I stumble against the wall of the building. Everything falls into place. Why Jason knows everything. Why he's here. Grammy. The bread. His condo.

"Nova? You okay?" Jason strides up, spotting the two phones. His face contorts. "Nova, let me explain."

"Is it true? You're Jace Pickle?"

He holds out his hands. "I needed to get answers."

I fling his phone at him. It lands on the ground with a crunch. "He's the owner," I tell the officer. "He can handle this."

I turn away.

"Nova!" he calls.

I don't hear anything he says after that because as soon as I'm three steps away, I run.

29

JACE

I'm not sure what to do. The officer keeps asking me questions. I can't go after Nova right now.

The woman sits on the ground, the colored lights flashing over the alley.

"So, does she work for you?" the officer asks.

"She's not a current employee. But she's either worked for me before, or she knows someone who did, because she had the keys and the combination to my safe."

The officer stills his pen. "Are you saying she was able to just walk into your place of business?"

"Someone's been stealing for months. We did an internal investigation to see if it was someone within the organization and determined it was not. We put an alarm on the back door to catch who was getting in. We also have camera footage."

"So, is it your intent to press charges against this woman?"

"Absolutely," I say. "We marked the bills in the safe tonight. They're probably on her."

Another officer takes a small knapsack from the woman. "Should I search this?"

"We'll let them handle it down at the station," the man says. "And what is your name again?"

"Jason Packwood," I say. "I'm known as Jace Pickle to match the name of the chain."

This will take some time to unravel. We'll need legal documents proving who I am.

"Can you come down to the station?"

"Let me call my lawyer," I say. "I guess I can meet you down there?"

He nods. We'll take her and book her."

He heads over to the officers surrounding the woman.

I pick up my phone from the ground. The screen is cracked. Figures. It still functions, thankfully, because I have to call Audra. I don't know who our lawyer is, just that we have one.

I walk in through the back door of the deli. I'll have to lock up here. I don't know if Nova is going to come in tomorrow. If she's going to quit. I may have to run the deli by myself for a while.

Frankly, I don't know where to go from here.

I wake up late the next morning. I spent hours down at the police station and, normally, I wake up either with Nova or with a text from her. I didn't set an alarm.

The woman, a friend of the old manager Susan, confessed immediately. However, she insisted it was only her second time to go in.

But she did tell the officers Susan told her they'd been doing this for months and not to worry. This was enough evidence for them to go after Susan. The investigation is only beginning. When the accountant provided documentation of losses exceeding seventy thousand dollars, the charges moved into the felony range. The whole matter became a big deal.

When I get out of the shower, I have calls from my assistant, the lawyer, and my father.

I return Dad's first.

His voice booms, and I have to hold the phone away from my ear. "What the hell's going on?"

"Nice talking to you, too, Dad."

"Don't give me any lip, boy. I've heard about a fired manager and major losses. And nobody down there even knows who you are?"

Apparently, he had spoken to Audra. Or Max.

"We'll file with the insurance. They'll investigate. The police are on it."

Dad hesitates for a moment, then busts out in a hearty laugh. "No wonder your books were so bad. You sure got yourself into a hell of a mess."

"I'll clean it up, Dad."

"You want me to come down there?"

"No. It's fine. We're handling it."

"I reckon you're going to stay there for a while and make sure everything's tied up?"

Like I have a choice. I may not have a manager anymore.

"I will. I've been here for a couple of months. I know how everything runs."

"Glad to hear you've taken some interest in your business. Maybe if the insurance kicks in, your losses won't be quite so bad this year."

Right. The competition. "I don't have a chance of winning," I say. "I'm trying to get everything under control."

"Well, your brothers and I are here if you need anything."

I skip the other two calls, instead quickly heading to my car. I need to get to the deli. It should have opened half an hour ago, but I don't know if it did. For all I know, Nova never showed up to unlock the doors.

But when I park out front, I'm somewhat relieved to see customers seated inside.

Kate and Lamonte work the lunch line. Nova has to be somewhere if they got in. I push through the door, but the moment Lamonte sees me, he breaks away to cut off my path.

"Is Nova here?" I ask.

"I told that girl you would break her heart. I had no idea it would be like this." Lamonte's withering expression could peel paint off a wall.

"You didn't answer the question."

Lamonte is undeterred by my attitude. "Nova isn't here. She called me, and I got the keys. I'm taking over the role of assistant manager until she can finalize it, I guess with *you*."

I look around the deli. A few customers have taken an interest in our conversation. Kate has her head down. She doesn't even want to make eye contact.

"Is Nova with her mom? She's not answering any calls."

Lamonte crosses his arms over his chest. "I don't think you'll be hearing from her. Look, we can run this deli without you. You take your fancy self back up to New York or the Riviera. You seem to like it best. And girls in string bikinis."

I grimace.

Lamonte snorts. "Yeah, I stalked Jace Pickle. I saw you with all those actresses. All the beaches. I don't think you've worked a day in your life."

"I did here."

"Whatever. You just move along. We'll get the locks changed. Nova said as soon as you're safely out of Texas, she'll come up and change the combination on the safe. You can scoot on out of here."

He takes a step toward me, aiming to escort me out the door.

"This is my deli. I could fire you."

"You assume we even want to work for you anymore? This is about Nova. She's got dreams, mister. She needs this job for those dreams. So, you get on out of here and let her live her dream. Let her make her money and go back to school. She doesn't need you, or anybody else to get it done."

Lamonte is right. If I stay here, Nova will quit. And that will set her back.

"Will you tell Nova something for me?"

Lamonte shrugs. "Maybe I will, and maybe I won't."

I plunge on. "Tell her I always intended to confess as soon as we caught the thief. I didn't have to stay here once we knew it was happening. I didn't want to go. I didn't want to leave her."

I catch Kate watching me before she quickly turns away. Lamonte doesn't say anything but moves over to the door and opens it. His response is clear. I need to get out.

And because it seems to be the best thing for Nova, I do as he says.

30

NOVA

It's been the worst week in a life that's had some pretty bad weeks.

Jason, or Jace Pickle, or however I'm supposed to refer to him, has called and texted.

I'm aware of how frustrating it can be to watch couples refuse to work out their differences, so I respond to a text or two with short simple phrases. *New locks installed. I am fine.*

Not that it changes anything.

He asked me if I could forgive him for the deception, and I told him there was nothing to forgive. He had a job to do, and he did it.

He asked if he could see me, and I said I'd rather not.

I almost typed that I was uncomfortable dating my boss, but then realized how hypocritical that was, given until the night of the arrest, I'd been *his* boss.

He asked me if it was about trust.

And that one hit me in the gut. Because, in the end, it really was.

I could see how this started. I remember the moment when he looked around the deli on that first day. In hindsight, it's clear he got this idea to figure out who was stealing from him by working here.

I don't find any fault with that. It was self-preservation. Or deli-preservation.

But we crossed a line in the freezer that day I showed him the mountain of cheesecake. And he knew it. That was the moment he should have said, hold up, there's something you need to know before we get any more naked.

But he didn't. And things went so much further. So much.

A man who can't figure out when to hit the brakes on a lie isn't a man I can trust with my heart.

Although, it's too late for that.

It's taken three days to pull myself together enough to get to the deli again. I knew Jace was gone. Lamonte kept me appraised of how the deli was running without me. They were a little shorthanded, and struggling, particularly to get the bread baked in the mornings, but they've managed.

Audra called the deli with Jace's approval of Lamonte's assistant manager position. She also authorized hiring not just someone to replace Kate next month, but a whole new position.

And that was smart. We did run better with Jason at the deli to help with the morning baking and the chopping.

The thought of him at the mixing table threatens tears again.

No. Stop.

I have to pull it together.

But it's hard. I still look around my office and struggle to reconcile what happened here.

And what will never happen again.

Jason Packwood. Laughing. Touching my knee. Doing so much more.

I brace my elbows on the desk, my head in my hands. I've shut off the camera in this room. It isn't necessary, and I don't need anyone hacking the system and watching me fall apart inside these walls.

I turn my head and glance at the taped-over window. We never did take those papers down.

Maybe I should.

I stand up to do it, but as soon as my fingers touch the tape he placed there, the waterworks start all over again.

What is up with this? I do *not* cry.

There's a rap at my door.

I hurriedly wipe my eyes with a Kleenex and toss it in the trash. "Come in."

Lamonte steps inside. "Lunch rush is extra heavy today. We could use you out there."

"Okay, I'm coming."

Lamonte pats my shoulder as we head out. "You need to engage with the world, Nova. Get back in the game."

I take a deep breath and try to prepare myself for the insanity that is Austin Pickle at lunch.

It's busier than usual. While I was out, Lamonte came up with the brilliant idea to solve the dessert problem, as well as reduced foot traffic during this wet spring. If it's raining, customers can get a free dessert, packaged in a cute little box, to take with them with any sandwich order.

After only three days of the special, we've made a noticeable dent in the freezer. And our average sales are up instead of down.

When we enter the main room, the line is out the door and curled underneath the awning. Out in the street, a steady, mist falls. It's a perfectly miserable day, the sort the makes you want to curl up on the sofa with a cup of coffee and try to console yourself.

But we have people to feed, and desserts to package. I move behind the register to get started.

The rain doesn't let up, so by the time I get home late that afternoon, I'm absolutely ready to curl up in a sweatshirt with a hot drink.

Leah sits at the kitchen table, math homework spread out in front of her. "There should be a law against replacing numbers with letters in math problems."

I lean over her shoulder. "They're teaching algebra in fourth grade?"

"My generation is so much smarter than yours."

I thump her lightly on the head. "I think we're the same generation."

Leah shakes her head. "No. You're old. And definitely dumber."

I head to the microwave to heat a cup of water. "What's with all the hate today?"

She twirls the pencil through her dark hair. "Oh, I don't know. Maybe somebody mooning over some dude like there isn't a million fish in the sea."

"I thought you liked Jason."

Leah rolls her eyes in that particularly charming way known only to elementary school kids. "I did until he broke my sister's heart."

Mom walks into the kitchen just in time to hear Leah's pronouncement. "Did somebody break my baby's heart?" She pulls a previously opened bottle of wine from the cabinet, but I shake my head *no* at her. It can wait until Leah is in bed.

"That Jason boy from work," Leah says coldly.

Mom frowns but sets the bottle back on the shelf. "Who is this boy?"

I don't want to admit he's the owner. "A guy from work. He moved back to New York. That's all."

Mom gets all interested. I steel myself for one of her random acts of mothering. She presses both her hands to my cheeks. "My baby. How is it I don't know about this man?"

Probably because she doesn't pay a lick of attention to anything but her own life. But I simply say, "He was only in town for a little while."

Mom's eyes search my face. "So, this is the reason you didn't come home a lot?"

Leah's head pops up. "She's setting a terrible example for her impressionable little sister."

I reach down and thump her head again. "It's different when you're a grown up."

"Back to your homework, Leah," Mom says. She takes a step back from me. "A man who can't stay through thick and thin is no man for the heart of my daughter."

"He was never meant to——" I cut myself off. Why am I defending him?

"You know I'm right." She trails her fingers through Leah's hair. "I have made terrible choices in men, but they gave me two wonderful daughters. So for that, I can't hate them."

Both Leah and I snap to attention. Mom never talks about our fathers.

I only know my father's name because I saw it when we did the paperwork for my driver's license. I immediately looked him up.

Married for twenty years. And I was sixteen.

When I confronted her with what I'd found, she said, "Some men will promise you the world and leave you only with ashes. A man like that is not worthy of being the father of my children."

I've never contacted him, although I looked at pictures of his other kids for a year or two. Eventually, I graduated and lost interest in the sperm donor I'll never know.

Leah's father is an even bigger mystery. Mom made up the name on Leah's birth certificate, a problem we'll eventually have to deal with.

But not today.

As usual, considering my mother's problems makes mine seems small. So what if a temporary love affair ended like it was supposed to?

But the way my eyes prick tells me otherwise.

"My water's hot," I say, headed for the microwave.

I dunk a teabag in the cup and head to my room, where I'll get a blissful bit of alone time while Leah finishes her homework.

Living with my entire family at twenty-two is definitely no picnic. I have zero privacy, but I'm committed to providing stability for Leah until she graduates high school.

Eight more years. Then I'll be thirty.

Like Jason. Jace.

I force myself to focus on my tea, reveling in the steam rising to my face.

I'm surviving this. It might not be easy. But it's probably for the best. The one time we tried living in his world, I bailed before we got to the maître d'.

Men like Jace Pickle simply aren't made for girls like me.

31

JACE

I thought two weeks on the Riviera would be amazing. A return to my old life.

The beach is just as white. The water is blue, and all the old cronies I always hang with are there, ready to party.

But none of it works.

The girls all seem flimsy, like paper-thin versions of themselves. They purr and preen, and if the littlest thing goes wrong, like too much bleu cheese on their salad, they crumple.

None of these people work or do anything meaning-ful. They couldn't slice an onion if it smashed them in the head. They can't imagine spending hours on a single loaf of bread.

Still, I play along, going through the motions of my old life.

But one day Amanda Schilling sidles up to me in a string bikini that can barely claim its existence. She wants me to snap out of it. She knows exactly how, running her fingers along the waistband of my board shorts.

I awaken from my stupor just enough to picture Nova in her camo pants and Army boots. The vision comes hard and takes over every sense. I have to will it away, almost physically striking the air to make it leave.

But when Amanda leans in to whisper, "What do you think is the sexiest scent in the world?" I can't stop myself.

I turn to her with all sincerity and say, "Pickle juice and bread dough."

Her face contorts. "That's just weird." Then she adds, "Gross."

And that's when I know I've had enough. I snatch up my shoes and clomp through the sand to my beach condo.

How has this one Texas girl wrecked me so hard? I can't enjoy anything I did before.

I toss my shoes by my front door and head for the sliding glass doors on the other side. I'm on the third floor, and the balcony looks out over the water and an endless expanse of sand. It's a perfect place to sit and think.

I can't seem to go back to where I've been. I'm not that person anymore.

The ocean pounds, wave after wave, crashing through sunbathers and breaking across the shore. As the day goes on, I quit answering messages from my lazy, do-nothing friends. They seem to have no interests other than what bar they will visit that night and whose famous Instagram they might land on. I program my phone to send them all directly to voicemail, and their texts all get silent alerts.

Done.

And it's quiet.

My life goes on this way. I sit alone most nights on that balcony, hypnotized by the waves. I sleep here and there, occasionally ordering take out or a pizza. I don't know what to do. What I *can* do. I'm not sure who I am anymore. Jace Pickle, part of my father's delicatessen world? Jason Packwood, a real person, who makes friends with the employees of his business? Who does manual labor, and gets to work before dawn?

I'm certain no one's noticed I've disappeared from the world until one afternoon, about three weeks after I've left Texas, somebody knocks on my door.

I have no idea who it could be. My friends don't come here. I didn't order anything. The cleaning service isn't due for a few days.

The person I absolutely do not expect to see is my brother, Max.

"What the hell?" I ask.

"Nice to see you, too, bro," he says.

I haven't seen him since the hospital at the baby's birth. His body is even more tricked-out than before.

I take a step back. "Are you on steroids or something?"

Max's expression hardens. "Now see, that's about the biggest insult you can give to a bodybuilder. So shut the fuck up about that."

I turn away to flop onto a chair. "Sure. Sorry. I didn't expect to see you."

Max steps inside and shuts the door. "You look like shit."

"It's not been my best year."

He plunks down on my sofa and picks up a pizza box to set it on the floor. "You're even worse off than we feared."

"Did you fly all this way to give me a lecture? Don't you have a deli to run? The competition to win?"

"Anthony's kicking both our butts. It doesn't even matter to me. I'm starting the circuit soon, so I won't have much time to mess with pickles."

I wave my hands at his rippling physique. "You're going to go pro with that?"

"When my coach says I'm ready. But I'm not here about that. It's all about you."

I tug at my T-shirt self-consciously. It's the *Keep Austin Weird* one. I'm not quite sure when I changed it last. "So, you see me. Clearly, I'm fine. Did you want to go get a beer or something?"

"We could do that. But you haven't been answering messages from anybody. Dad thought you'd like to know what's happened with the investigation into the theft at your deli."

I kick my feet up onto the coffee table, pushing aside a half-filled container of fried rice. I have no idea how old it is. "Yeah? It's all done?"

Max leans forward, clasping his hands together. Damn, he's huge. He's like two of me now.

"They caught up with the old manager. She pled not guilty at the hearing, but then she decided to take a deal. She had an arrangement with the old assistant manager to skim cash and cover it with inter-deli deliveries."

"That's what Nova figured out." Even saying her name draws a shard of pain through my gut.

"Yeah, Dad talked to her. She said you had mostly figured it out and were trying to catch whoever it was."

I try to picture Nova and Dad talking. My throat gets tight. "So, was the lady we arrested the old assistant manager? She said she only went there twice."

"No, she was new. The old assistant manager got spooked when Nova took over. She felt like they milked that cow for all it was worth. But Susan wanted to keep trying. She got the old assistant manager to turn over the keys and combination to another friend."

I rub my eyes. I don't want to think about this anymore. "Sounds like it's all wrapped up. The deli will be fine, just like before."

"Dad wants you in New York," Max says. "I'm to get you on a flight sometime this week and head to the main house."

"And if I don't go?"

"I have the muscle to force you."

He did have that. I didn't expect he would literally throw me over his shoulder and haul me onto a plane.

But I guess the Riviera plan wasn't working out anyway.

I might as well go to New York.

Just not Texas.

32

NOVA

The email from Sherman Pickle feels like a bad dream.

I read the words a second time, an icy tendril of fear trickling through my veins.

To: Nova Strong, Andre Williams, Marie Rodriguez

cc: Jace Pickle, Max Pickle, Anthony Pickle, Lance McAllister, Audra Wilson, Bud Miller

I don't know the names of most of these people. I recognize the Pickle brothers, obviously, and I can only guess the Audra listed here is Jace's assistant.

I read on.

. . .

We are long overdue for an in-house meeting of owners, managers, and top personnel of the Pickle franchise. Audra will be coordinating flights and accommodations for everyone to meet the first week of June in New York. Please plan accordingly with your staff to be away for approximately five days.

Bud Miller, our accountant, will be contacting you regarding any additional materials he may need to present budget findings. We will also be meeting with our lawyer regarding the events at Austin Pickle, and how we can best protect the franchise from future loss of assets.

I look forward to seeing you all again, and meeting those of you who are new to the upper management of our beloved delicatessens.

Sincerely, Sherman Pickle.

I have to go to New York.

Well, I *get* to go to New York. That's exciting. I've never been to New York.

And here is an all-expenses-paid work vacation.

Will I get to see the Statue of Liberty? Rockefeller Center? Will I have time? Can I afford side trips?

Despite the excitement, I keep going back to a name on the list.

Jace Pickle.

He'll be there. The cold feeling of dread comes over me again. I can't see him. I probably shouldn't even be working here anymore. Except, I need this job. And I love this job. And I love the crew I've built. And there's nowhere else I can work up to manager as fast as I did here. It was a lucky circumstance. I know those don't come along very often.

No. I need to hold out for a year, then I can go back to school.

But now there's this trip. And Jason. Jace. Whatever.

"Ho, ho. What's got the boss lady all upset today?"

It's Lamonte. I should've kept my door closed. He always notices when I'm in distress.

He stands in the doorway. Now that he's assistant manager, he likes to wear short-sleeved shirts with collars. I find it amusing. He also reinstated the employee pins when he read in the manager manual that it was the duty of the assistant manager to provide them.

I think he just wanted one with his name and *assistant manager* on it.

"I have to go to New York," I tell him.

"What!" His tone is something between disbelief and jealousy.

"Sherman Pickle is having all the managers come in, plus the franchise staff. We'll have to talk about the theft and how to prevent it from happening again. Plus, budget stuff."

"You think they're gonna blame you for old Susan?"

"I don't think so. Most of that was set up before my time."

"How long will you be gone?"

"He says five days."

"Good thing we hired that new person. We'll be fine without you." He leans forward and peers at the screen. "Just make sure I have all the phone numbers I need in case something breaks down. You'll be gone right when the new pickle of the month arrives. I'll get the signage done and start the promotion."

I had to hand it to Lamonte. Give him responsibility, and he shines. He is five hundred percent the employee he was before.

"I'm not worried about you guys."

"It's Fancy Pants, isn't it? He will be there."

"His name is on the list. I assume they'll make him come."

"What will you do when you see him?" Lamonte asks. "I think it's a close race between a withering stare…" He models one, which makes me crack a smile. "Or the classic." He takes a step back and then lunges forward, fist out. "A punch straight to the nose."

I shake my head. "I'm hoping I have enough time to see a few sights and pick up something for Leah."

He plunks down into a chair. "Oh man, you gotta see all the good stuff. The statue. Ellis Island. Top of the Rock." He continues listing tourist attractions, and I'm about to ask if he's been to New York when another email comes through on my official manager address.

It's Audra, asking how many days I want to come up for.

"What should I tell her?"

He peers at the email. "She says to give her dates. There are three days of meetings, but you can go a day or two early and stay a day or two after." Lamonte turns to me with an evil grin. "They're paying for the hotel. Take all the days, baby."

It would be nice to have a vacation. I've never had

one. And they are paying for the hotel and flight. I would have to cover food on the extra days, though.

"I don't want this to get crazy expensive," I say.

"Eat hot dogs from the carts," he says. "Refill your water bottle. Take a big box of granola bars for breakfast. You can do this, girl. Walking in Central Park is free. Sitting on the red stairs doesn't cost nothing. You can get half-price tickets to the shows on the same day they play on Broadway. Do this, girl!"

I laugh. "Okay, okay." I type in an arrival date for two days before the meetings, returning two days after. An opportunity like this might never come again, at least not until I'm through with school and have a professional job where taking business trips might be the norm.

"Done." I hit send.

Lamonte lets out a whoop. "You have yourself the best time. Now what are we gonna do about clothes?"

I look down at my pink camo pants and Army boots. "I have to go to school, Lamonte. I can't spend a bazillion dollars on new outfits."

"Hush. The first outfit's on me. Let's hit the thrift shops."

"Let's get this deli closed first," I say. "I have a few weeks till I leave. We can shop."

When Lamonte has left the office to start the process of shutting the deli down for the day, I turn back to the email. Seven days in New York. And Jace Pickle will be there too.

I don't know what it will feel like to see him again. It's been a month since he left, and by then, even more time will have passed. I glance out into the empty kitchen. The crew should be starting to break down the sandwich line.

I stand up and quietly close my door. When I turn back to my computer, I open the Internet and type in the name I've avoided since he left.

Jace Pickle.

The hits stream down, and images line up across the screen. Unlike typing his birth name, the electronic data on Jace as the owner of the deli franchise merits pages and pages of information.

There's Jace and his two brothers, plus father Sherman, who sent out the email. The most popular pictures are at fundraisers and gallery openings, Jace in suits and tuxedos.

He does make formal clothes look good.

Then there are tons of pictures of him with other women. Girls in gowns or slinky club dresses. There's an entire Instagram feed that seems to center on him at the beach. The French Riviera, according to the tags. Despite the sick feeling I have that I'll see him mugging with some other woman, I click through to look at them.

This feed is owned by a woman whose profile picture makes her look like a supermodel. Long blond hair, perfect white dress, tilted straw hat.

The images I'm initially led to are months old, before he came to Austin in March. Jace is the quintessential party boy in them, arms around men and women alike, laughing, always dressed in smart, perfect outfits that fit each occasion. There are club pictures, beach pictures, sitting at sidewalk cafes. My heart hurts looking at his perfect face.

One is a closeup of him in pale-blue swim trunks. I trace the lines of his abs, the muscles of his chest, my finger gliding along the screen. I remember his body so well. I bite my lip to stuff down the emotion that threatens to well over.

The party pictures go on without him during the two months he's here. I hold my breath as I reach late April, when he left.

And he shows up again.

But it's not the same. Gone is that easy, open expression. He sits apart from the others. He doesn't show up in the club pictures, only the beach ones.

And within a few days, he's missing again.

Did he go back to New York?

I click through some of the tags and find another woman's feed. She seems to fancy herself as an artsy photographer, so there are tons of individual portraits of this circle of friends. She has many shots of Jace. In most of them, he's looking out at the ocean, or sitting by a fire pit, partially lit by orange light. She titles them, "Brooding Jace" and "Jace lost in thought."

He disappears for her, too, confirming he must have left the Riviera. But as I'm about to leave her feed, I see an odd picture that makes me click through.

It's the side of an apartment building, balconies overlooking the curve of the beach. It's shot from the ground, looking up, and centering on a figure standing on a balcony three floors up.

I can't make out who it might be from the image, but

the caption on it makes my throat tighten. "Our lost Jace. Wishing he'd come down from his tower of torment."

The date says it was shot only a week ago. So, he hadn't gone away.

He just left the scene.

I press my hand to my chest as I realize he's hurting as much as I am.

33

JACE

This franchise meeting is bullshit.

I've owned Austin Pickle for eight years, and we've never had one. The case against my former manager, and the two women who were accessories to her theft, is practically closed. They all took deals to avoid a jury trial. They got off easy, if you ask me.

In fact, I can't exactly figure out what Dad wants out of this meeting in New York. It's too early for him to announce the winner of the brother battle, unless maybe Max and I are so far behind Anthony we can't possibly catch up.

Or maybe since Max wants to become the next Mr. Universe, or whatever, and I have royally screwed my chances of winning, he's going to call it early. Spare us all the trouble.

Regardless, it's going to be torture sitting in the same room as Nova.

Her brief, professional responses to my early messages were worse than being ghosted. Everything she wrote told me she wouldn't ignore me, but the only thing between us now is the manager-boss relationship.

I have to be fine with that.

Dad tries to insist I stay at the same hotel as everyone else. He's bought out the floor of one near Manhattan Pickle and expects everyone to stay there to be available for meetings and brainstorming sessions.

But I don't. On the day of the first official gathering, I wake up in my own Midtown loft, flicking through a lengthy list of outraged messages while I brush my teeth.

Six are from Dad, increasingly incensed, asking why I'm not at the hotel in my room.

Three are from my brother Anthony, asking why I can't do this for Dad.

One is from Audra, asking if I want to use my afternoon time slot for a private meeting with the accountant and my manager Nova. I tap out a quick *no* to that.

And one from Max, saying if I don't show up, he's going to haul my ass there himself.

I don't really want him to show up at my place, so I quickly message him that, yes, I'm coming to the meeting, I just didn't want to go to that stupid dinner last night.

I don't know what I will say or do around Nova. If she maintains the same strict professionalism with me in person that she has with her messages, there's no point in doing or saying anything other than *thank you for your service*.

I have to hold it together.

I put on six different outfits, seeing each of them through Nova's eyes.

Too pretentious.

Too stupidly expensive.

Show off.

Poser.

In the end I wear the Pickle shirt she gave me and top it with a plain white short-sleeved button-down, left open. It's Austin style, not New York, but at least it silences the criticism in my head.

I appreciate New York traffic, driving aggressively and taking any excuse to lay on the horn. I feel pent up, angry, pissed off at the world that any of this happened. That I found Nova. And lost her. And I can't get her back.

Even the hotel valet elicits a negative emotion, remembering when Nova got so out of sorts at that fancy place I foolishly took her to on our first date.

I practically lunge from the car, stalking into the lobby of the hotel without so much as a glance at anyone.

I'm a walking New York cliché. But I can't do anything about it. It's going to take everything I've got to get through this without a stupid outburst.

I summon the elevator, realize I can't get to the private floor without a security card, and head to the front desk. I'm feeling irritated about having to stand in line when I hear a voice that steals my breath.

Nova.

I turn in slow motion, eyes darting through the expansive lobby, searching for her face.

She emerges from the hotel restaurant with none other than my brother Max.

Awesome.

Max's voice booms across the lobby. "And there he is. My brother Jace."

"So even you guys call him Jace?" Nova asks.

I know what's coming.

Max explains. "Jason insisted on it. Apparently, some girl that my dear brother pulled his love 'em and leave 'em act on created a MySpace page for Jason, the evil killer from Friday the 13th, and plastered it with pictures of Jace."

I hate this story. I try to get out of earshot, but there's a damn line, and the two of them walk closer. I remember Elena Price and her Jason page. Only when MySpace finally fell out of popularity was I able to escape that stupid association. I was in college at the time, and things like that fake page really got to me.

I made everyone start calling me Jace. And by the time I was listed as the owner of Austin Pickle, Jason Packwood was pretty much no more. He died before Facebook took off. I was more than happy to live as Jace Pickle by then, so everything I'm on these days says I'm Jace.

Only Nova calls me Jason now.

I don't hear them talking anymore, and I assume they've headed toward the elevator. I refuse to look their way, so the punch on my arm catches me by surprise.

They're right beside me. Max and his tricked-out body-builder frame.

And Nova. My eyes can barely graze her, noting the haircut, layered around her shoulders, a green sweater I've never seen before, and the pair of black dress slacks.

New things. Clothes I've never peeled off her. Will never peel off her.

"Max," I say with a nod. I meet Nova's gaze only for the briefest second before I turn back to the line. "Nova."

In my peripheral vision, I spy Max shaking his head. "Forgive my brother, Nova. He doesn't deserve you."

My jaw tightens. Does he know we were a thing? Did Nova tell him? No one should know outside of the old crew.

"He did good work when he was in Austin," Nova says. "He ended up making bread better than me."

My chest relaxes as I realize she's not letting on that we were more than just coworkers.

"What'cha standing in line for, bro?" Max asks.

"I need an elevator key," I say, fully aware my voice is closer to a growl than conversation.

"Somebody got up on the wrong side of the pickle jar," Max says. "Dad's got plenty of key cards upstairs, including the one to your room. If you'd been at the dinner last night, he would've handed it to you. Come on."

I do not want to follow Max and Nova to the bay of elevators, but I have no choice. Inside my gut, everything is roiling like I'm a volcano, ready to spew lava over the land.

While we wait, Nova says to Max, "I don't think I ever properly thanked you for my raise and bonus. The first time I heard you speak, I realized it was you I talked to that day."

She doesn't even glance my way.

Max beams at her. "Anybody can see you're the best thing that's ever happened to that crappy little deli in Austin." Then he takes Nova's hand and tucks it in the crook of his arm.

What? Was he moving in on Nova? Had they been seeing each other since she got here?

I do not pause even a moment to think I might be wrong, or this isn't what it looks like.

The red flares up behind my vision, and before the elevator even arrives, I shout, "Hands off her, mother fucker."

And I plow my fist into his jaw.

Oh no, oh no, oh no.

As Jace's fist connects with his brother's face, I spin to come between them.

"Jason!" I shout, forgetting that he's Jace now. "Stop!"

Max, who easily outweighs his older brother with fifty pounds of solid muscle, barely flinches from the blow.

But either Jason doesn't hear me, or he doesn't care, because he swings a second time.

I duck to miss getting hit myself and ram my head into Jason's belly.

Jason stumbles back, and I lose my balance. We both tumble to the glossy floor.

Jason's arms come around me to soften my blow. I land on his chest, but as soon as we're both down, I scramble to get away from him.

"Damn it, Jace," Max bellows. "Why the hell do you have to make a scene?"

He reaches down to pull me up by the hand. "Are you okay, Nova?"

Jason leaps up with a roar. "Keep your hands off her."

I whirl around him. "What has gotten into you? He was helping me up."

"Don't touch her," Jason growls again, eyes on Max.

Max holds up his hands. "I don't know what you think is going on here, bro, but you can back the fuck off."

A tall man in a black suit approaches. "Is there something I can assist you gentlemen with?" He's completely composed for someone walking up to a brawl in his posh hotel.

"We're fine," Max says. "We're heading up to our floor."

The elevator has opened and closed since this alter-cation began. Thankfully the lobby is fairly empty mid-morning.

"We're okay," I tell the man. This is more than I bargained for.

Jason looks out of sync with the rest of the hotel in his Austin Pickle shirt and jeans. For possibly the first time I've ever seen, he is the least dressed-up person in the room.

I try to sound soothing. "Jason—Jace, I mean. Let's go upstairs. The first meeting has probably already started."

Max takes my arm again, and his threatening look tells Jace he better back off.

Still, I unravel my arm from his. "I'm okay. I can walk on my own."

The three of us load into the elevator, sullen and quiet.

Max has been super great since my arrival in New York. He and Audra have shown me around town, taking me to restaurants and getting us private visits at some of the big destinations, including the Metropolitan Museum of Arts, and parts of the Rockefeller Center closed to tourists.

It's been a fantastic two days, but I know what Jason saw when he spotted me and Max together at breakfast. A closeness he didn't expect. A breakfast date that suggests maybe something else had happened.

I decide to just get it out. "I'm not sleeping with your brother," I tell Jason. "I wouldn't do that."

Max makes a strangled sound. "What?"

I glance up at him. "We were seeing each other in Austin. It didn't end well."

Max clears his throat. "That explains a lot. We knew he was wrecked. I guess we should've known it wasn't someone from his usual crowd."

Jason stares sullenly at the wall, his fists tight like he's trying not to punch something else.

We arrive at our floor. Jason follows behind us as we head toward the meeting room at the end of the hall. We're late, but since I'm walking in with two of the brothers, I don't worry about it. Jason is my boss, and if I'm with him, then I'm probably where I'm supposed to be.

Sunshine flows through the windows onto the long

conference table. I met most everyone at the dinner last night. Sherman, the father, and Anthony, the youngest brother, stand as we enter. Audra gives me a little wave. There are several men I don't recognize, and I assume they include the accountant and the lawyer, since all the managers were at dinner last night.

I sit down next to Audra. She leans in. "What happened to Max's face?"

"Jason."

Audra's eyes widen. "You'll have to tell me later."

I'm not sure I want to, and I'm glad for the distraction of the meeting. The brothers settle into seats near the front of the table. The distance from them is a relief.

The hard part of this week has begun.

Sherman remains standing. "I trust everyone is having a lovely stay in New York," he says. "I wanted to call this first meeting so we could discuss some of the things that have happened in the franchise, and to also look at the direction where we're headed as we go into this new decade."

He introduces a man named Dell Brant, who has the female managers sighing as they admire him in his fitted gray suit. He definitely commands a room.

But I spot him frequently glancing toward the back corner. I follow his gaze to a curly-haired woman bouncing an energetic toddler on her lap. The two of them share a smile, and my jealousy is pricked. I remember those stolen glances with Jason.

Dell gives a rousing speech about corporate culture, taking risks, and pushing the envelope. Everyone sits a little taller and leans in a little closer to catch his every word. I see why Sherman wanted him to give us a pep talk.

Jason sits back in his chair with his arms crossed, carefully keeping his eyes away from my end of the table.

When Dell finishes, the meeting goes on with reports from the accountant and spirited conversations about pickle and bread recipes.

I'm asked to talk about what happened with our former manager, and how we uncovered her actions and what we have done since to protect the business. I'm careful not to accuse Jason of being an absent owner that allowed it to happen.

I swear I sound shaky, but when I'm done, Audra squeezes my wrist and says, "You did great."

When the attention is no longer on me, I steal a glance at Jace. He's focused on the notepad in front of him, drawing circles in a lazy pattern all over the sheet. I'm not sure he listened to a word I said.

The meeting breaks for lunch, and Audra leads me over to the other managers. "I thought you all might like to talk shop without the bosses around," she says. "I arranged for a catered lunch in one of the suites for you guys to kick back until your private meetings with your owners."

I grab her arm. "Do I have to meet privately with Jace?"

She shakes her head. "He turned your meeting down."

I don't know if I'm relieved or disappointed.

The managers head to their rooms to drop off their

notes before reconvening. I walk down the hall and spot the woman with the toddler sitting on a bench outside. Dell chats with Sherman a little farther down the hall.

"Who is this?" I ask.

"Grace," the woman says. "She's eighteen months going on twenty. She wants her independence."

As if to prove the point, Grace lunges from the woman's lap, almost launching away. "See?"

I press my hand to the toddler's back to help right her. "I have a younger sister. I remember when she was like this."

The woman wraps her arm around the little girl to extend a hand. "I'm Arianna. Dell's wife."

I shake it. "I wondered. He kept looking at you."

Arianna's face pinks up. "I like watching him speak. We do most things together."

My throat wants to close up. "That's nice."

She tilts her head. "I saw you looking at Jace. You're his manager, right?"

I nod. I don't know what to say beyond that. We've just met, and only Max knows about me and Jace, and that only since this morning.

"I couldn't help but notice he was watching you, too, when you weren't looking."

He was?

"Forgive me if I'm overstepping, but I sense something more than an owner-manager relationship."

My belly flips. Are we that obvious? "There might have been a bit more."

She glances down at Grace. "You know, when Dell and I met, we had this real love-hate thing going on. It took a hard split for us to realize how perfect we were for each other."

"But he's my boss."

"And Dell owned my building." She laughs. "We had a real mess of a situation." She holds both of Grace's hands as the little girl dives backward and grins at me upside-down.

"Our situation is pretty messy, too."

"There's obviously a lot of feelings between you two. Sometimes a problem can seem insurmountable, but then somebody gives just a little bit."

Grace gurgles, spit bubbles forming between her lips. She finds them hilarious and lets loose with a hearty toddler laugh. I'm already smitten with her.

Audra walks up. "Ready, Nova?"

I tuck my notebook into my bag. "Yes. Nice meeting you, Arianna." I touch Grace's nose. "And you too, little monkey."

Grace giggles.

I try to put Jace from my mind for the next hour. The lunch with the other managers is fun. We joke about the names of the breads, and generally complain about staff turnover, which seems like a constant battle. Despite my being new at my job, the others treat me as an equal. I've never felt so important or respected.

We take a tour of the Manhattan Pickle, and I'm amazed at the size and scale of this deli compared to ours.

Their sandwich line is easily three times the size of ours, and even in mid-afternoon, when we would be shutting our deli down, this one has a line to the door. A full twenty employees rapidly take orders, prepare sandwiches, and man three cash registers.

By the time I get to my room in the evening, I've decided to stay in. I want to be alone with my thoughts and recover from seeing Jason again. Had he really thought I would take up with his brother? Could everyone see what Arianna saw?

I change into sweats and a T-shirt and try to watch some television, but all I can think about are the images I saw of Jason on the Riviera, and his contorted, emotional face as he attacked his brother.

He's no better now.

I'm not going to blame myself. He was the one who lied. Who hadn't owned up to his lie. I've been careful and professional.

I think about texting him, but I don't know what to say. I wonder if he's staying here tonight, or if he refused again.

Not that I'd know which room is his.

Not that I'd go if I did.

Would I?

I allow myself a moment to remember his mouth on me, the dozens of scenes playing out in the pantry, the freezer, my office, his car, his condo.

This can't be a throwaway love affair.

I feel too much.

It's overwhelming.

I walk over to my door. Is he so close I could go out into the hall and scream his name?

And if he was, would he come to me?

What is he doing right now?

A piece of white on the floor catches my eye.

It's a piece of paper.

The hotel stationary, like what we were using in the meeting.

It's folded in half.

With shaking fingers, I lean down to pick it up.

Audra would have texted me. Or Max.

There's only one person who might slip a note under my door.

My heart bangs painfully as I open the page.

There are only four words.

Can I come in?

35

JACE

I stand outside Nova's door for what feels like ten years.

Maybe she's not even in there. I know she's not off with Audra or Max because they are downstairs in the bar with the family. I went down there for all of thirty seconds, planning to turn and leave when I bumped into Grammy Alma.

I gave her a big fake smile and a hug, trying to avoid crushing her plumped up gray hairdo that seemed half spun from air.

But she smacked my shoulder. "Don't you fake it with me. Max told me all about you and your sweet manager."

"Are you going to give me a lecture about fraternizing with my employees?"

"Of course not. She's perfectly delightful. Kept us all entertained at dinner last night. The one you skipped."

"It's hard to be around her." It felt good to admit that.

Her face softened, the hard lines of eighty years fading into her warm expression. "Well, I only have one thing to tell you."

"What's that, Grammy?"

She smiled the mischievous grin I've known all my life. "Room 2408."

I stand here looking at the numbers now. Nova still hasn't opened the door.

I wouldn't open it either, not after the shitshow that was me and Max earlier today.

A shadow moves at the base of the door, visible in the narrow gap where I shoved the note. It's her feet.

I lean against the cold steel. She's so close. When I flatten my hand against the surface, I can almost imagine hers is on the other side. Only two inches of metal separate us. But it's enough.

"I can't fix what I did," I say to the door. "But I can promise you I'm different. I know what we had is damn rare. And even if I screwed this up forever, I'm grateful you got me off the pointless path I was going down."

I lean my head on the door. "You're the real deal, Nova Strong. I feel lucky to have known that for a while."

The other side of the door is completely silent. I wait a minute or two more, then realize there's no point standing here until someone shows up to witness my pathetic bid to get her back. In a world of grand gestures, flash mobs, skywriting, and full-scale productions to declare your love, my little note is nothing.

I don't deserve her. Soon, she'll be on her way to a promising future, past my deli, back at school, and on to bigger and better things. I'll the chump sitting in my condo watching her TED Talk.

She doesn't need me.

"I've said what I needed to say." I step away from her door.

I don't plan on staying at the hotel. Knowing how close Nova is, and not being able to be near her, is too much. Now that my family knows what happened between us, I think they'll back off. They're nothing if not a bunch of romantics, and they know how deep hurt can go.

I should have been more like them all along.

I take about five steps toward the elevator when Nova's voice stops me in my tracks.

"Hey, Fancy Pants."

I bite my cheek so I can control my expression as I turn around.

Then I realize, no. That's what got me in this problem. Deception. An unwillingness to take a risk.

I move toward Nova with my heart out, all my feelings on my sleeve. I'm willing to take whatever she's going to dish out. It's her turn to throw a punch. I deserve it.

She stands in her doorway, bathed in soft light from her room, dressed in gray sweatpants and the pink T-shirt I recognize from Dad's deli. It reads, "I'm done dillin' with you."

"Are you?" I ask. I stop a foot away, close enough to smell the shampoo in her hair.

She looks at me quizzically.

I reach out and trace the letters below her collarbone.

She glances down. "Oh!" Then she sobers up. "I don't know. I thought I was done."

"But now?"

"I'm not so sure."

Our gazes hold. I see in her all I've missed these last weeks apart. Her beautiful face, framed by glorious hair, and the intelligence in her expression. She is so much better than me at… well, just about everything.

She lets out a long gust of air. "I stand corrected."

"On what?"

"Your pants. They're not fancy."

"Old Navy, off the rack."

"Those jeans would *not* pay the rent."

I'm happy just to have a conversation with Nova. Any conversation. But there are so many things I want to know.

"So, is there a chance for me?" I watch her face closely, looking for clues.

Her lips press together. "You lied to me. We had an entire affair going on, and you were lying to me the whole time."

"I was scared," I say. "I was so fucking scared. What we were doing was so perfect. And I wanted to wait as long as I could before I screwed it up."

The elevator dings, and Nova's eyes go wide. We have the whole floor, so it will be someone we know.

"Quickly. In here."

She grabs my arm and pulls me into her room.

When she closes the door, she leans against it. Everything I'm feeling competes for my attention. Relief, that we're talking. Joy, that I'm so close to her.

And other thoughts, because she's clearly ready for bed.

And there's a bed.

In the room.

I back up and bump into it, falling to sit awkwardly on the end.

"You okay?" she asks.

"No."

She sits next to me. "I don't bite."

"You probably should."

She tucks her hair behind her ear. "What do we do, Jason?" She hesitates. "Do I have to call you Jace?"

"No."

"Good."

"Why?"

She shakes her head. "I don't know. Jason feels like who you were with me."

"I want to be that man. I am that man."

"But are you still scared?" Her eyes search my face.

"Hell, yeah. I'm scared shitless."

"Over me?"

"Over losing you. Over not getting to love you. Over never feeling the way I feel about you again. Never loving anyone like this again."

I can't take it anymore, and I pull her to me, cradling her head on my shoulder. I'll keep it easy, nothing she won't want. But I need her close, so I can feel her, smell her, know one more time what it's like to hold her in my arms.

We're quiet for a bit, then she says, "Are you saying you love me?"

I won't hesitate on this. It's my only shot. "I do."

Nova pulls away. "Then why didn't you tell anyone? Why did you lock yourself up in that condo on the beach?"

So, she looked for me. Found information on where I was. She cared enough to do that.

My heart hammers hard, like it maybe—just maybe —has something to beat for again.

"I didn't know how to fix this. Fix us. I texted you. It was no good."

She falls silent, looking down at her hands. "Should it be fixed?"

I pick up her hand and lift it to my lips. "I'll do anything to fix it."

Her eyes meet mine again. "Remind me why we were so good."

I squeeze her hand. "Well, we always had things to talk about and—"

My head knocks sideways as she smacks me with a pillow. "Shut up and *show* me."

She's smiling. Nova is smiling at me and it's like the world has broken open with light.

I don't make her ask twice and pull her close to me. My mouth falls on hers, and every sappy love song I've ever heard fights to win dominance in my head. It's birdsong and sunrise and birthday cake.

I feel like my heart will burst.

But I have work to do here. Nova needs to know what makes us work. The proof.

And I am the man for the job.

I run my hands through her hair and down her back. I find the bottom of the Pickle shirt and let my thumb run gently along the warm skin of her belly.

Her breath makes its first uptick in speed, and I have her. She's mine now. I turn her so I can lift her up and move us to the center of the bed. I will worship every part of her, take my time.

And love every minute of it.

I spread her hair out across the pillows and slowly inch the shirt up over her ribs. I kiss every fresh reveal of skin as I go. When the shirt catches on her nipples, I slowly inch it over those taut buds.

Then they are mine, succumbing to my hands and mouth. Nova arches her back. I tug the shirt over her head to land across the room.

She's bared to me, and I feast on her, lost in the sounds she makes, the warmth of her skin.

I push down the sweatpants, my fingers grazing her thigh, her knee, her smooth calf.

When she's in nothing but panties, I lift away to look at her.

"This is the only vision I ever need," I whisper and her brown eyes lock on mine.

I grasp the panties and ease them down, feathering kisses on her hips. I spread her knees wide and dip my tongue precisely on the bud of her clit.

Her body lifts to me, and I clutch her, diving deeply, revisiting all my favorite places. Her muscles tighten, her legs framing my face. I gaze up at her, those glorious breasts arched high, her hands clutching the pillow.

She's mine, and I remind her how we work together as the pulsing in her body begins.

"Inside," she says. "I want you. Inside."

I shuck my clothes as fast as possible and crawl over her. "This?"

"Yes. I want to see you."

I brace myself over her body, emotion flooding me. "Hey, Nova," I say.

She stares up at me, my face above her. "Yeah?"

"I love you."

She lifts her head to press a quick kiss on my forehead. "I know."

I slam inside her, and she quickly tones her scream down into a gasp. "Your Grammy!" she says. "She's next door."

So that's how Grammy knew Nova's room.

But I don't slow down, circling Nova's clit with my thumb. Nova tries to keep it down, but as I lean down to take her nipple into my mouth, she lets loose, her cries rattling the lamp on the side table, her body writhing beneath me.

I let go inside her, and our bodies pulse in tandem. I'm on top of the world, having crested the highest mountain, the hard part behind me. I've reached the summit of everything.

Nova lets out a small sob, and I gather her against me. Is she regretting this already?

"Nova?"

"I missed you," she says. "I missed you and I hated missing you. You make me weak."

I hold her tightly against my chest. "I missed you, too. And I was weak."

My shoulder grows wet and I hate I ever caused her to cry.

"We can fix this, can't we?" I ask. "I'll spend my life trying to fix this."

She wraps her arms around my neck. "You can. You will."

I rock us back and forth on the bed, reveling in how close we are right now.

Not all broken things are lost. Sometimes knowing how fragile they are makes you realize their importance.

And we are definitely stronger after a fall.

36

JACE

You can *think* you're fooling the Pickle family, but in reality, you can never actually fool the Pickle family.

Even though Nova and I carefully orchestrate a five-minute delay between when she and I walk into the first meeting of the morning, everybody seems to know.

For one, they played a joke on us. While I was busy tucked in bed with Nova, dear old Dad changed the start time of the meeting from ten a.m. to nine-thirty.

This means that Nova and I, who were paying attention to absolutely nothing but each other's naked skin, missed the texts and emails about the change.

So, we are both very late.

Which makes our situation quite obvious.

Grammy sits at the head of the table with Dad. When she sees me, she starts a slow-clap.

The managers and staff don't seem to be in on it, but of course they follow her lead.

Max's expression is pure snark, and Anthony shakes his head with amusement.

Dad doesn't clap, but stands with his arms crossed, looking from me to Nova, and back to me again.

I sit down between my brothers.

For a moment no one speaks. Finally, I say, "Are we having a meeting or is everyone just going to stare at my impressive good looks?"

The table laughs, and I glance over at Nova, hoping she isn't mortified. She shrugs.

I realize I don't want to be this far from her and stand up again.

"Audra, let's switch places. I need to sit next to the most amazing woman in the room."

Audra hops up immediately as eyebrows raise throughout the meeting space.

Grammy Alma slams her hands down on the table. "And I assume you mean after me."

I squeeze Grammy's shoulders as I walk around. "Of course, Grammy. Of course."

I sit down and take Nova's hand in front of Dad and everybody. No secrets. No more.

That night Dad arranges for karaoke in the bar downstairs. When the managers seem hesitant to get up and sing, Anthony kicks it off with an impressive low-throated version of Louis Armstrong's "Hello, Dolly."

This breaks the ice, and two of the Manhattan

Pickle managers take their turn singing, or rather, shouting, old Beastie Boys.

I sit in the corner with Nova, holding her hand.

As a third group heads to the microphone, Max drags a chair over to our table.

"This is a table for two," I say. I know I should probably apologize for punching him yesterday, but we're brothers. And brothers have a whole different set of rules.

"Well, you stole my girl. It's only fair I should get to sit next to her now."

I kick him under the table, and he laughs. "Jace, bro, you are too easy." He turns to Nova. "So, I was thinking about singing a soulful duet about love. Jace won't get up there. He's too cool for karaoke. Will you sing with me?"

Nova's eyes get wide, looking back and forth between me and Max. "I'm not sure I'm a big karaoke singer."

"All right. Then I guess I'll have to sing to you."

I kick him again. "Damn it, Max. What the hell are you doing?"

"What I do best." He stands up and claps me on the back. "Making you look bad."

Max takes off to go speak with the woman running the karaoke machine.

Nova takes a chug of her drink. "So, do you boys really hate each other, or is this some weird brotherly love I don't understand. I do only have a sister."

"It was always weird growing up. I was the big

brother. Max was the most outspoken one. It made for a bit of a rivalry."

"Anthony seems like the softy of the group."

"Yeah, he's the only one with any sense. We ought to be looking up to him."

"Max said something yesterday about a competition for the franchise. Will it affect Austin Pickle if you lose?"

I shrug. "We all get to keep our own delis. Mainly Dad's looking for a successor for the big Manhattan store, as well as control of the chain. Anthony already runs everything. He does the pickles of the month and the breads and all the clever stuff. It only makes sense he should win."

Nova squeezes my hand. "Are you going to come back to Austin to run your deli?" Her voice is tentative, as if she hasn't had the courage to ask this question all day.

I bring her hand to my lips. "Of course I am."

"I'm staying here through Saturday."

"Then I'll get a flight back Saturday. I suppose we can spend some time running around New York if Dad's done with us."

"I think tomorrow is a Pickle breakfast at the deli. Then we have the rest of the day."

"I can think of a lot of good uses for that time."

The song ends and Max steps up on the tiny stage. "Everyone let's welcome to the stage our favorite brother with a special song to the love of his life, his manager Nova Strong. Jace, come up here and sing to your lovely lady."

Everyone claps and turns to my table. "Oh, shit," I breathe.

"Can you carry a tune at all?" Nova asks.

"I don't know. I guess. But I'm not really a singer."

She nudges me. "I think you need to get up there. You owe it to him for punching him in the face."

My hands tighten into fists. But Nova's right. I decided I would take risks. Be a new man. Open up my feelings.

Why not start with shame and ridicule?

I scoot out from behind the table and another cheer goes up from the crowd.

Everyone is there. My dad, my brothers, Grammy. All the managers. My cousin Sunny has showed up. In the back I even spot Greta, pressing baby Caden to her chest inside one of those baby wrap carrier things.

I wind my way through the tables, quite ready to murder my brother in front of a live audience.

But I don't. I stand next to him.

"Break a leg," he says.

"What fresh hell have you come up with for me?" I ask.

"You'll see."

I look out on the crowd of family, business partners, and friends. I have to step up. I'm making up for a lifetime as the big brother, the big cousin, the pain in the neck who bossed everyone around and judged them for being not cool enough.

I stayed away, too much of a legend in my own mind to be a mere deli owner.

Now it was time to be humble.

And as the opening chords of the song begins, and laughter ripples across the room, I realize something.

They got me good.

Before the first words can start, I find Nova in the dim light of the bar. "This one is apparently from my family to you," I say. "So here I am, singing it just like you'd want me to."

Another whoop goes up, and then it's time for this Big Pickle to sing his own self-absorbed anthem:

"I'm Too Sexy."

And to sell it, I throw my shirt at my girl.

37

NOVA

Three Months Later

Lamonte spots me coming out of Bertha, a sack of flour under each of my arms.

He halts in his tracks. "Nova, what are you still doing here? You're gonna be late!"

"I have to make sure we have enough ingredients. Samantha is new to making the bread. We're not used to having to bake it all day. Everything is different!" I hear the strident note in my voice and try to take a deep breath.

"Aisha!" Lamonte calls. "Come here and help Samantha make the next round of bread." He takes the bags of flour from me and places them on the mixing table. "Nova, we've got this. You get yourself to campus."

He's right. We do have this. Four new employees.

Arush has been moved up to a second assistant manager. I've become a figurehead now that Jason is here every day.

Business is way, way up, and Jason is even looking at buying out the building next door to expand.

It's been a wild rush since the beginning of summer and the implementation of all the new ideas we brought from the New York meeting. Jason and Anthony have been thick with plans, and now Austin Pickle is open through dinner as well as on Sundays. It's been a huge adjustment.

But that's not my problem at the moment. I have to get to campus. It's the first day of the fall semester.

And I'm back in school.

I unlock my cubby and pull out my backpack. "You know the procedure to shut down the register and balance the receipts?" I call out to Lamonte, who is watching Samantha measure out ingredients.

"Boss lady, I could do that in my sleep. Now scoot on out of here."

I sling my backpack over my shoulder as Jason comes out of the office. "Hey. You ready?" he asks.

"You don't have to drive me. I can grab the bus."

He kisses the top of my head. "Of course I'm driving you."

We push through the swinging doors and into the front. Despite the craziness in the kitchen, we are in the afternoon lull. The staff is preparing for the dinner run.

I pass behind the sandwich line, checking the supply levels out of habit. The cheddar's low, but I'm sure

Lamonte or Eli, who is manning the line at the moment, will spot it.

Jason and I head out the front door into the bright, beautiful fall day.

"I'll go grab the car," Jason says. "Save your walking legs for campus." He takes off for the garage before I can argue.

I wait under the bright green-and-white-striped awning of Austin Pickle. The sun streams down, reflecting on the clear shiny windows of the deli.

My life changed here. It gave me a stable place to work while I supported my mom and my little sister.

It provided me with job experience and an accidental promotion that will only help me as I finish out my business degree.

My throat tightens as Jason's BMW pops out of the garage a few blocks down and he waits for an opportunity to turn onto the street.

Austin Pickle gave me the love of my life. Since Jason's return, our time together has resumed as it should have always been. I split my nights between his condo and the apartment with my mom and sister.

I still love my work and my crew.

And now I get to continue this amazing new adventure with a degree in hand. That starts today.

Jason pulls up next to me and leans over to open my door. "Can I give the beautiful lady a ride?"

I lean down to peer at him behind the wheel. "Is my innocence safe with you?"

"Absolutely not."

"Then I'm all in." I slide onto the leather seat.

Jason reaches over to grab my hand. "Nervous?"

"Not in the least."

"Good."

The city blocks whiz by as we leave downtown for campus.

It's not my first time going to school.

But it is the first day I can really picture a bright, beautiful future for myself. I have a job I love, a man I love, a family doing better than they ever have in our lives.

So even though the ride got a little bumpy along the way, today feels like a brand-new perfect beginning.

EPILOGUE

Reckoning day has come.

It's New Year's Eve, and Dad has called us all up for a gala he's hosting, plus the announcement of which brother has earned the most money this year.

The situation has not been a complete secret. Every quarter, the accountant provided all of us with the numbers for each of the delis so we could stay aware of our standing.

I have to admit I'm pleased that all the extra work we put into Austin Pickle since summer means I have charged ahead of Max. It wasn't that difficult, given that L.A. Pickle has remained a lunch-only restaurant while I have followed Dad and Anthony's lead in becoming full-service.

The final quarter has remained a mystery, though, and the results will be revealed tonight.

Nova emerges from the bathroom of our hotel room, and my breath catches.

She wears a full-length black beaded gown, long-sleeved and glittering. The square neckline shows plenty of cleavage, and when I let out a low whistle, she turns around to show me the back, or lack thereof. There's nothing but skin from her beautiful neck all the way to her waist.

She looks delectable, the most entrancing woman I've ever seen. No one could hold a candle to this, no A-list actress or runway model. Not even close.

She glances over her shoulder. "Given the status of your fancy pants, I think you like what you see." Her smile is pure mischief as her gaze drops to my crotch.

"No spreadsheet folders to cover it," I say.

She laughs. "I forgot about that."

"I still can't see a pair of cowboy boots without thinking of it."

"That was our first day in the freezer."

I nod. "The beginning of everything."

She turns to me and taps her finger on the lapel of my tux jacket. "Also, the beginning of when you should have told me who you were but didn't."

Nova brings this up regularly. I get it. She wants to keep me honest. I draw her close and press a kiss to her hair, all done up in a fancy swoop. "And you should absolutely never let me forget it."

"Don't worry. I won't." She grins up at me, but when I lean down to kiss her lips, she scurries away. "Don't mess up my makeup. I paid a lot of money for this!"

"So that's where you were all afternoon."

"Sephora," she says. "The poor girl's makeover."

Nova is still fiercely independent, paying for her

mother's apartment as well as school. I love this about her, but I'm constantly trying to think of ways to help.

As she sits on the end of the bed to slide on her heels, I finger the velvet box in my pocket. I'll find out tonight exactly how entrenched that independence is.

But I want her to be my wife. I want her challenges to be my challenges. Her struggles, my struggles. When I had it easy, I nearly threw it all away. Nova saved me from that, and she showed me what was most important.

And now I have everything.

Nova stands, kicking up a heel to reveal the red underside of the black shoes. "I still can't believe you got me these for Christmas. I could've paid—"

"A month's rent with these, I know." I take her hand in mine. "I appreciate your frugality and common sense very much. But every once in a while, it's nice to splurge."

"All right," she says. "But you know it only makes me want to go back to that hotel in Austin and rub these fancy shoes in that wicked lady's face."

"She doesn't hold a candle to you," I tell her. "And there will always be people out there trying to make you feel small. Letting it go means you will always be bigger than them."

"Wise words from a Pickle," she says. "Are you ready to go down?"

I hold out my arm. "Ready if you are."

I might be the Big Pickle, the eldest, the bossy one who always acted nonchalant when faced with problems. But as we head down the elevator to the ballroom where Dad will announce the winner prior to the official Pickle New Year's Eve party, I'm nervous.

I'm not sure how I will feel if I beat out my brothers. Or if I lose.

And I'm not sure when, or even if, I'll get up the nerve to propose to Nova. This is the most unpredictable evening I've faced in my life.

As Jason heads onto the small stage with his brothers and father, I shift uncomfortably in the chair next to Grammy Alma. I've never been to an event this fancy, and most of this family I barely know.

Only three of the tables are filled at the moment, and the sea of empty ones tell me the size of this party will be quite overwhelming when it's in full swing.

The tables are gorgeously decorated in black silk with green and silver centerpieces. Even though they're not exactly pickles, the color scheme and the clever arrangements evoke the feeling of the delicatessen franchise. It's well done.

I turn the stem of my wine glass around and around in my nervous fingers as the brothers laugh and cajole each other up on stage. Apparently, they will sign papers almost as soon as the announcement is made. Then the Pickles will have their own private dinner, and afterward the actual gala will begin.

Grammy Alma leans in. She smells of lilacs, and her bracelets jingle as she gestures toward the stage. "Don't all my boys look so handsome up there?"

"They sure do."

She adjusts the neckline of her gray silk dress. "This outfit is way too fussy. Surely, by my age, I can show up wearing a flour sack if I want to."

"I feel you," I say. "I say next year we all wear Pickle shirts and jeans."

"You're my kind of girl," Grammy Alma says. "I hear you've gone back to school."

"I still have three semesters left."

"I don't know if anyone has told you how pleased we are that you're part of the family."

I want to contradict her. I'm just a girlfriend.

But she holds up a hand. "I've known baby Jason all his life. He's been a wanderer, a free spirit, a rebel. But now look at him."

Both of our gazes are drawn to Jason in his tux, elbowing his brother Max. The boys jostle, almost as if they are eight years old and trying to be in the front of the ice cream line.

"He was hardly ever here, gallivanting off to the beaches and clubs." She gives me a wink with a blue-eye-shadowed lid. "I know about Instagram."

I give her a small smile. So, I'm not the only one who's stalked Jace Pickle.

"But now he's down there with his franchise, doing well for himself. That's on you."

"I don't know about that. He comes from a delicatessen dynasty." I elbow her lightly. "That's on you."

"I only led the horse to water."

The two cousins Sunny and Greta hurry in from the back door. They're both decked in elegant dresses, although Greta looks harried, shoving bobby pins into her updo even as they traipse across the empty ballroom. Sunny's long hair swings as they rush to the front.

Behind them is Jude, Greta's husband, holding baby Caden, who is nine months old and determined to squirm out of his arms.

The women drop into chairs at our table.

"So sorry we're late," Greta says. "I tried to give Caden one more feeding before we came down."

"Can't let that baby go hungry," Grammy Alma says. "You're just in time."

Sherman steps up to the microphone. "Looks like we finally have everyone here." He smiles down at Greta and Sunny. "Including my favorite nieces."

Jude comes to sit at our table, but Greta waves him toward one of the others, where Sherman's brother Martin and his wife are waiting. Fran holds out her arms eagerly for her grandson, and Jude deposits the squirming baby into her lap.

Sherman gazes fondly at them. "One of these days, my sons will see fit to make me a grandparent."

I feel a number of eyes turn to me, but I keep my gaze fixed on Sherman. The idea of babies hasn't even crossed my mind. School first. Then the rest.

"Now that everyone is all assembled," Sherman says. "We will take care of a bit of business for the franchise. Most of you were in the room on the day the littlest Pickle was born, when I issued a challenge to my sons. The deli with the highest earnings by the end of the year would take over Manhattan Pickle, as well as control the franchise itself. This Pickle will direct all of the chain-wide activities and set the tone for the franchise."

He pulls a folded sheet of paper from a pocket tucked inside his suit jacket. "I have reviewed the numbers. Before I announce the winner, I want to commend all three boys for increasing their profits so dramatically this year. Maxwell, your deli in L.A. had twenty percent growth this fiscal year."

The family claps, and I let go of my death grip on the wineglass to join in.

"Anthony, who has been our most profitable spinoff deli since opening four years ago, had a remarkable fifty-six percent growth."

More clapping.

"My own Manhattan Pickle, despite seemingly maxed out in its ability to push through any more customers, had a modest nine percent growth this year."

Grammy Alma lets out a boo and the word, "Slack-er." The room breaks out in light laughter.

"Thanks, Mom. I know I'm a great disappointment."

The laughter increases.

"Austin Pickle, however, under the direction of a new manager," he gestures to me and I grip the wine-glass yet again, "and with increased hours and an extra day of the week, has had a remarkable one hundred and forty percent growth in revenue."

The applause for Jason is even louder, and Audra whistles between her teeth. This excites baby Caden, and he begins giggling and clapping his hands, setting off another ripple of laughter in the room.

"See, even our littlest Pickle approves."

"He's a Jones!" Jude calls out, shaking his head.

"Every Pickle's a Pickle," Sherman says, then waits for the room to quiet.

"So now we find out who was the most profitable. All the boys had gains, which is extremely noteworthy and fills me with pride. But the most improbable deli has come out victorious."

Improbable? Does that mean ours?

I watch Jason carefully. His face is a mask of calm, but he holds his hands behind his back, and I know they are gripped tightly.

We talked about this moment several times. He hasn't wanted to win it, although he feels the pressure of being expected to do so.

Sherman folds up the paper and tucks it into his pocket. "It is with great pride that I pass on the ownership of the original deli and control the franchise. With gross receipts that exceeded what my own deli made in its first decade in only a few years, this son has proven he is a tremendous businessman, and will steer the Pickle Empire into the next century with enthusiasm and competence."

He turns to the three boys, extending a hand to Anthony.

"Anthony Pickle, I entrust our franchise to you."

Anthony's face is pure emotion, and after accepting the handshake, he pulls his dad into a hug.

Everyone claps, including Max and Jason. I watch Jason carefully, trying to identify exactly how he feels.

The brothers shake Anthony's hand as well, and the

lawyer steps up on to the stage to draw Anthony and Sherman away to review a leather portfolio.

Jason steps down from the stage and returns to the chair beside me.

Greta reaches across the table to take his hand. "Over a one hundred percent increase?" she says. "That's phenomenal, Jace. Really outstanding."

"He's back to Jason," Grammy Alma says. "Thank God."

Greta smiles. "Good. I never liked Jace."

"Me neither," Sunny says.

Grammy and the two cousins stand up to go congratulate Anthony. I lean into Jason. "You okay?"

"I always felt Anthony was the best choice." He slides his fingers along the inside of my wrist. "We've got a lot on our hands in Austin already. I didn't need to be taking over the New York deli as well."

"Is Anthony going to split his time between Boulder and Manhattan?"

Jason shrugs. "That's up for them to decide. He leans back in his chair. "I'm glad this is done."

Servers bring out dinner, and the merriment of the family is apparent as everyone wanders between tables, eating salads at one spot, the entrée at another, and desserts at yet another place, mingling and talking.

I get to know Greta and Sunny better. I'm introduced to Martin and Fran, who holds a sleeping baby Caden on her shoulder.

Sherman drops beside us to let us know he'll be visiting Austin soon to see what he can learn from our expanded operation, and help oversee the expansion, since he's done it twice.

"I'm proud of you Jace—Jason," he says. "I hoped this competition would bring you around, and it did."

"Hogwash," Grammy Alma says.

"It got him to go down to Austin, now didn't it?" Sherman rubs his chin, seemingly perplexed at his mother's outburst.

"The accountant's figures got him down there," Grammy says. "It was Nova who got him interested in his deli."

Sherman nods. "I give. At least it worked for something. Now maybe I can retire. If only I had a grandchild to bounce on my knees."

"Hush up," Grammy says. "Go play with Caden and get your baby fix."

Sherman chuckles. "I think I might."

New guests filter in as the actual gala begins, and musicians set up on the stage.

Before long, the noise levels rise, and the band is playing. The New Year's party is in full swing.

"Want to dance?" Jason asks.

I nod and let him draw me onto the dance floor in front of the stage. A dozen other couples sway slowly together. It's a classical waltz, and Jason guides me smoothly across the floor.

"It was the right thing," Jason says.

"You mean the competition?"

"Yes. I've been thinking…"

He trails off, and I wait for him to expand on his thoughts, but he doesn't.

"Is everything okay?"

"What do you want to do, Nova?" he asks suddenly. "Do you see yourself running the deli even after you graduate? Are you going to want to move on?"

He misses a step in the beat, and I wait until we've resumed the rhythm before I answer. He really is anxious about this.

"I don't know. I haven't thought that far ahead."

His hand tightens on mine as we shift out of another couple's path. "I always had my destiny laid out for me. And I rebelled against it only to find it was exactly the right thing. But I'm open to change. I don't have to stay in Austin. I will never be as absent of an owner as I was for a while, but I don't have to be there."

"Just don't let the Susan situation ever happen again."

"I won't. But do you want to stay in Austin?"

I lay my head on his shoulder, letting the music move us as I think about this.

"I want to be near my sister until she graduates," I say carefully. "That's another eight years. I'll be done with school in less than two, so I assume I'll work somewhere in Austin for those six years. Are you telling me I won't always have a manager's job waiting for me?" My heart hammers. Now that he's lost the competition, does he want out? To leave? To leave me?

"Of course you do. I just wanted to get a bead on where you thought you were headed."

I lift my head to look in his eyes. I don't see anything alarming there, a need to escape or tell me hard truths about our future.

My belly settles. "I think it's New Year's Eve, and we are at an amazing, glamorous party hosted by your own family, and these things can wait for another time."

He relaxes at that, and I know it was the right thing to say.

The song ends, and we part to clap along with the other dancers.

"Let's get away from the noise for a bit," Jason says.

We wander hand-in-hand through the ballroom and out the side doors. A large tiled balcony overlooks Central Park. Despite being quite far away from the craziness of Times Square, the revelry here is apparent, with a nonstop flow of pedestrians walking along the sidewalks and clumping around the carts still open along the streets.

I shiver despite my long sleeves, and Jason wraps his arms around me. "We don't have to stay out here long."

"I'll be okay for a minute. It is beautiful."

"I try not to take any of this for granted," he says. "In fact, I don't take much of anything for granted."

"It's a good way to live."

He squeezes me, his chin on my shoulder. "I love you, Nova Strong."

I turn around in his arms. "And I love you, too. Sentimental tonight? Is it the competition? The fact that we're here in New York?"

He stares into my eyes. "I've been caught up in this idea that I should do big things. Grand gestures. Fireworks, barbershop quartets, and synchronized dancing. But I feel like that's old Jace. Not who I am now. But I can't seem to get past it."

I press my hands into his cheeks. "Good Lord, Jason, what are you talking about? You know I'm not a showy person. I'm not big on being on display or going viral or showing up on everyone's Instagram feed. I don't need ten thousand likes to know something important has happened."

My knees tremble. I think I've figured out why Jason is so nervous tonight, why he keeps pressing me about my plans now the competition is over.

"So, what makes a special occasion special to you then?" His eyes are earnest on mine. He really wants to know.

I look out over the park. "Seeing beauty all around me." I look up at him. "Being with the person I care about the most."

He bites his lip. "Then maybe this is the perfect moment."

My heart hammers. He's going to do it.

"Nova," he says. "Wait. Let me start over."

I giggle. "Start over with what?"

"I'm supposed to get down on one knee," he says.

Now I'm laughing. "So why aren't you?"

"Shit. I'm screwing this up." He pushes his hair off his forehead. "And I just said *shit* during my marriage proposal."

Now I'm laughing so hard I don't think I can give him a straight answer even if he does ask. "Are you proposing?"

"Yes. No. I don't know."

I force myself to sober up. "All right, Jason. If that's

your intention, let me step away. That'll give you the opportunity to pull yourself together."

He lets out a long breath. "Okay. Take two. Pretend you don't know anything."

I turn around, my hands clasped together like a Southern Belle in an antebellum movie. "Oh, what a beautiful starry night. It's New Year's Eve and the gardens are so beautiful." I may have even added a little southern twang I usually suppress at all cost.

"Nova?" Jason's voice has a nervous note to it.

I turn around. Jason is down on one knee, and he holds up a black velvet box, cocked open to reveal the most outrageous diamond I've ever seen in real life.

"Jason?" I am honestly aghast. This whole vision in front of me is hard to believe. Jason's beautiful hands, holding up this gorgeous ring. His tuxedo. His anxious expression, as if I could ever say no to him.

Greta's voice cuts through the quiet. "Oh my God! Is Jason proposing to Nova?"

"You better hurry up," I tell Jason. "I think they're on to us."

Jason turns his head, but it's too late. Greta has led a contingent to the ballroom doors. "He is! He is proposing! Get out here, quick!"

The partygoers quickly pile up at the doors. A million cell phones lift, some of them snapping photos with flashes, others set to video.

"I think you're getting your big moment," I say. "You better make it a good one."

Jason's gaze never wavers. "Nova Strong, love of my life, the most perfect, beautiful, strong woman I've ever known, will you do me the honor of being my wife?"

I take a step forward. If this is going to go viral, I might as well throw in a product placement.

"Jason Pickle, eldest brother of the Pickle Delicatessen Dynasty, love of my life, maker of dill dough, creator of dreams, I would be delighted and honored and so very lucky to be your wife."

Jason's eyes shine as he stands up and pulls the ring from the box. He slides it onto my finger and draws me into his arms.

"I guess I have to kiss you in front of all these people," he whispers against my cheek.

"Think of it as a free advertising opportunity," I say.

He smiles against my cheek. "Nova, you are the best thing that's ever happened to the Pickles."

"I only want to be the best thing that's ever happened to yours."

He drags me against him, and his mouth lands on mine. A great cheer rises up from the ballroom. Flashes rain down on us.

The voice of the emcee, amplified over the sound speaker, breaks through the applause. "Time for the countdown. Say it with me! Ten, nine, eight…"

The crowd returns to the ballroom as waiters scurry to provide last-minute champagne to the revelers.

We have the balcony to ourselves again as the last seconds of this crazy year tick down to a close.

When the cheer goes up, and fireworks start somewhere in the distance, Jason draws me against him. "This has been the best year of my life," he says.

I wrap my arms around his neck. "Mine, too."

"Do you think it's ever going to get better than this?"

"It doesn't have to," I say. "It only needs to be just as good."

Thank you for reading Big Pickle!

Were you intrigued by Dell, the Pickle family friend who recently acquired an unexpected newborn? Read my romantic comedy Single Dad on Top where the billionaire bachelor gets a baby — *instructions not included*.

BOOKS BY JJ KNIGHT

Romantic Comedies

The Accidental Harem

Big Pickle

Single Dad on Top

MMA Fighters

Uncaged Love Series

Fight for Her Series

Reckless Attraction

Get emails or texts from JJ about her new releases:

JJ Knight's list

ABOUT JJ KNIGHT

 JJ Knight is one of the pen names of six-time *USA Today* bestselling author Deanna Roy. She lives in Austin, Texas, with her family.

If you would like to see everything Deanna writes, here are links to her pen names:

JJ Knight
(Romantic comedies and MMA sports romance)

Annie Winters
(Romantic Suspense — slightly hotter on the scale)

Deanna Roy
(Emotional New Adult romance)

facebook.com/jjknightauthor
twitter.com/deannaroy
instagram.com/deannaroyauthor
bookbub.com/profile/jj-knight

Made in the USA
Coppell, TX
06 April 2020

19119212R00174